Fearscape by Nenia Campb

DEDICATION

To all the "nice guys."

You're underrated.

Fearscape by Nenia Campbell

Chapter One

It was one of those days in late April when the weather wasn't quite sure whether it wanted to be hot or cold, and so settled for a cloudy, muggy hybrid of the two. In Derringer, California, this meant stifling humidity and a windchill that made people think twice about removing their sweaty jackets.

Out on the high school's track, Valerian Kimble had already made the conscious decision to knot hers around her waist. Sweat was dripping down her face, blurring her vision and making what was left of her makeup run. During meets like these, Val was immensely grateful that boys and girls trained separately.

Her eyes flicked to the bleachers where a few students sat reading or talking, or waiting for the football team to come out and start their practice. Most of the spectators weren't even spectating. Track wasn't a spectator sport, not really. If you weren't participating, it wasn't all that fun. Who wanted to watch a bunch of teenagers run in a circle, over and over?

Well ....

One person did come to mind. But she wouldn't let herself think about that — not out here, with the wind in her

FEARSCAPE

by NENIA CAMPBELL

Fearscape by Nenia Campbell

Copyright © 2012 Nenia Campbell

All rights reserved.

hair, and the silvery light of a cloud-blocked sun shining bright in her eyes. This was no place for shadows.

"Looking sharp, Val!" Coach Freeman said, as she passed.

"Thanks," Val panted. "How did I do?"

Coach Freeman looked at her stopwatch. "We're at seven minutes now. So I want to say six-forty? Why don't you go ahead and take ten."

Sounds good to me. Val took a long drink from the fountain and then plopped down on the wooden benches in front of the bleachers. She was uncomfortably aware of her sweat-soaked shirt as the wind reasserted its presence. She untied her jacket and pulled it on, shivering a little as she pulled her hair out from behind the collar.

"You did good today, Val." Lindsay Polanski sat down beside her with a loud sigh. "What did you get?"

"Six-forty. You?"

Lindsay made a face. "Seven-ten."

"That's still good. Better than most people. And didn't you get six-fifty last time?"

"Yeah — and my stupid boobs nearly murdered my back."

"What's this about murder?" Rachel Lopez demanded, squeezing in on Lindsay's other side. "You guys planning something I ought to know about?"

"Breast reduction surgery," said Lindsay.

"Oh, like when you forgot your sports bra?"

Lindsay glanced over to make sure the coach wasn't watching and then gave Rachel the finger.

Rachel grinned. "Well. I bet it did wonders for our ticket sales. I think you made a lot of fans out there in the bleachers that day. There was one guy staring so hard, I thought he was going to burst a blood vessel."

"That is disgusting. Don't even joke about that."

Like the shadows beneath the bleachers. Val shuddered.

They watched the other girls on their team finish up. Some were red-faced and had switched over to a brisk power walk. Coach Freeman didn't shout at them to "hurry it up now, or am I going to have to use a calendar to keep track of you?" the way Coach Able might have back in middle school, but Val suspected that most of those girls probably wouldn't be coming back next year, in any case. Track was all about survival of the fittest; if you didn't clock, you walked.

Fearscape by Nenia Campbell

"Were you the first to finish?" Rachel asked curiously.

"Who? Me?" Val said. "No. There were, like, five others who lapped before I did."

The last girl—a natural blonde with ruddy features, who was wheezing a little — finally finished and Coach Freeman stopped her timer. "All right, girls — that's it for today. Go ahead and dress down, and take the rest of the afternoon easy. You've earned it."

The girls trundled like zombies, circling around the exercise gym and then cutting through the oak-shaded expanse where the skaters sometimes practiced their 180s on the concrete ramps. Juniper bushes surrounded the adobe-colored buildings, their thick, spiny foliage a magnet for spiderwebs, old leaves, and rodents. As she passed, the leaves rustled as some small creature wriggled its way through the tightly interlocked roots of the plant.

"I saw a rat in there once," Lindsay said, following Val's gaze.

The face that peered out at them through the leaves wasn't murine, though, but feline. A small tabby kitten blinked large eyes at them and mewed piteously. Val dropped to her knees, unmindful of the dirt, old gum, and dead leaves. "Well, hello." She wished she had some food.

"Rabies, Val," Rachel warned her, shaking her head. "It's wild. The janitor is always chasing the mother away from the cafeteria dumpster. She's mean."

"Forget it, Rach." Lindsay sighed. "She's completely ga-ga. You know how she is."

The kitten's hackles rose, and it puffed up like a little ball. It backed away from her outstretched hand, baring tiny fangs. Val lowered her hand back to her sneakers and waited. It was incredibly cute. She was pretty sure she'd seen the mother cat Rachel mentioned. Some boys had been throwing rocks at her. If she was mean, it was because she'd learned that she had to be, and not by choice.

"Bye, Val," Rachel said, her voice distant now.

Val ignored her. "Come on, cutie. I won't hurt you."

The kitten took a tentative step forward. Its paws were white, as if it had just walked through powdered snow.

"That's right. Come on. Look at you. Such a pretty kitty."

A sound, probably an acorn falling from the oak, cracked through the silence like a gunshot. The kitten retreated into

Fearscape by Nenia Campbell

the bushes as fast as greased lightning, and did not come out.

The wind curled through the branches of the oaks, causing the leaves to rattle together, and a few more acorns fell, hitting the macadam with a sound like knuckles popping. Val jumped. She thought she saw something move from the corner of her eye; a sinister wisp of black, slipping soundlessly behind the gnarled trunk of one of the old trees. She caught her breath, looking around — and found herself alone.

"Weird," she muttered to herself, taking another quick look around. The creepy sensation of being watched clung to her with a sticky tenacity as tangible as a spiderweb. She shivered and hurried toward the locker room, which had mostly emptied out now. With a final backwards glance, Val got to her feet and headed for the lockers. She stopped at the restroom first, though, to wash her hands — rabies, indeed. She splashed her neck and under her arms before returning to the locker room to change back into her regular clothes.

Lindsay and Rachel were on their way out when Val encountered them in the hallway. Lindsay was holding her car keys. Both of them grinned when they saw her. "Did kitten come out to play?" Rachel wanted to know.

"Almost. It was too scared."

Lindsay chuckled. "You and your animals."

"She *is* an animal," Rachel said.

"Humans are animals, moron."

"I know, that's what I was getting at."

They shoved each other as they walked, Lindsay turning over her shoulder to wave and say, "See you tomorrow!"

"Right," Val agreed.

And then she was alone. Her footsteps echoed as she walked across the stone floors — stone because it was easier to clean, she supposed — and past the rows of lockers which stood sentry like an army of metal gravestones. Combinations locks hung from each, silver with a red dial. The names of the lockers' respective owners were written on strips of peeling masking tape, last name first, posted at the top of the locker.

Val found more than just a lock ornamenting hers. Someone had left a single red rose sticking through the ventilation grates on the door. A card fluttered to the floor on paper as pale and weathered as a dead leaf as she cupped the head of the bloom in her palm. In an elegant hand that slanted rather violently to the left, someone had penned:

Fearscape by Nenia Campbell

Take me to you, imprison me, for I,
Except you enthrall me, never shall be free,
Nor ever chaste, except you ravish me.

Her fingers tightened around the stem and one of the thorns pierced her finger. A drop of blood soaked into the creamy paper, as if sealing it with an unspoken promise.

Who is this from?

And were they still here? Watching?

She thought of the black flash she'd seen out in the deserted courtyard, of the shadows she'd seen in the corner of her eye at school when she was alone. *Or maybe not so alone, after all.* Val bit her lip, opened the locker, and shoved her clothes into her backpack. *There's nothing there. I'm taking these home, but there's nothing there.*

A sound echoed somewhere close to the door. It could have been water rushing through the pipes, or it could have been a brush of movement against one of the lockers. She stepped backwards, hugging her backpack to her chest, and then she jumped as the icy metal of her own locker permeated the thin material of her track uniform like a cold finger running down her spine.

"Hello? Is someone there?"

Silence. Then she heard the sound again, softer this time, as though toying with her. She couldn't tell whether it was a figment of her imagination or real. She thought she might hear breathing. It was enough to make her explode out of the locker room, back into the concrete clearing. Very faintly, carried on the chill-touched wind, she swore she heard laughter.

No. She zipped her backpack shut with a rough jerk and raced out of the locker room on legs that were only slightly shaking. She threw the rose into the garbage. She felt bad for a moment — someone had spent money on that — but she shrugged off her guilt. *It's their fault for spending money on such a stupid practical joke.*

And if it wasn't a joke?

Then someone will own up to it, she decided. *Maybe.* She kept the note, just the same. She had no way of knowing that her actions were being monitored — and silently approved of. As Val walked to the parking lot where her mother was now waiting to pick her up a figure stepped out from behind one of the oaks. A long-fingered hand lifted the rose carefully from the trashcan, neatly severing the blossom from the stem with two fingernails, before secreting the flower away into the pocket of a black trench coat.

■□■□■□■

A white '77 Camaro came close to colliding with Mrs. Kimble's champagne-colored Honda Civic as she attempted to maneuver her car out of the school's parking lot. She laid on the horn, much to Val's embarrassment, as the old car raced past. "Idiot," her mother said emphatically. "That poor car, getting abused like that. It won't last long with that driver."

Val picked at her cuticles and said nothing, letting her mother rant. Which she did. At length. Until she remembered herself and asked, almost absently, "How was practice, Val?"

"Good," said Val. "I beat my time from last week."

"That's wonderful, honey. What was your time?"

"Six minutes and forty seconds," Val said, pride creeping shyly into her voice.

Mrs. Kimble laughed. "I wonder who you got that from. Your father wouldn't run if he were a computer, and Lord knows I never did better than a nine minute mile. Even at my prime." She shook her head mournfully. "Which was a long, long time ago."

"Nine minutes isn't so bad, Mom."

"Please," her mother said. "I'm an old tortoise."

"No you're not — I think you look great!"

Val's mother cut her eyes at her daughter. "That's very sweet. What do you want?"

"Nothing. I was just — " Val broke off when she realized her mother was laughing. "So not funny," she mumbled, folding her arms and glaring out the window.

"I'm sorry. That was wrong of me. What do you say to some coffee to celebrate your victory?"

Val peeked at her mother. "Can I have a large?"

"You can have," her mother said, with finality, "Whatever you want."

■□■□■□■

One visit to the drive-through later, Val was walking through her front door and up the stairs to her bedroom with a green tea frappuccino. She paused in the doorway for a beat, regarding her room with a faint smile. As cliché as it was, her bedroom was her sanctuary. White carpet, white walls, with a fluffy pink comforter that was as soft as a cloud. Bookshelf pushed up against the far wall, beneath the window, with all her favorite classics from a childhood that wasn't so long ago filling up the bottom-most shelf. A pile of CDs stacked haphazardly on display beside her computer — Kelly Clarkson, Tegan and Sara, David Cook, and Michelle Branch. A pile of CDs hidden away in her closet, but not dusty — 'N Sync, Britney Spears (all of them, except for the eponymous album), and a handful of artists featured on Radio Disney.

Yes, she was home. Safe.

And yet, in the pocket of her track shorts the poem was burning a hole, whispering at a threat Val didn't yet understand. Her smile faded as she looked it over a second time. The poem was too good to be the work of a student — Val knew this instinctively, having read far too many of her friends' own creations, most notably Lisa's. She suspected it had been ripped from somewhere. Most likely the internet.

Time to find out.

She set her drink on her nightstand, dumped her backpack in front of her closet, and then sat down at her computer. To narrow her search she encapsulated the lines of the stanza between quotation marks. To her surprise, she achieved results far more quickly than she thought she would. The poem was an excerpt from a work by John Donne, a contemporary of William Shakespeare in Elizabethan England. It was entitled Batter My Heart:

Batter my heart, three-person'd God, for you
As yet but knock, breathe, shine, and seek to mend;
That I may rise and stand, o'erthrow me, and bend
Your force to break, blow, burn, and make me new.
I, like an usurp'd town to'another due,
Labor to'admit you, but oh, to no end;
Reason, your viceroy in me, me should defend,
But it is captiv'd, and proves weak or untrue.
Yet dearly'I love you, and would be lov'd fain,
But am betroth'd unto your enemy;
Divorce me 'untie or break that knot again,
Take me to you, imprison me, for I,
Except you enthrall me, never shall be free,
Nor ever chaste, except you ravish me.

Fearscape by Nenia Campbell

The site listed some other works, as well, and Val read the first couple that were listed. She enjoyed *The Prohibition* the most. The others were either too confusing to understand, or so dark that she didn't want to grasp the meaning that lay behind them. Batter My Heart fell into both categories, but especially the latter. 'Imprison me?' 'Never be free?' 'Ravish?' These words and phrases evoked violent images that made her shudder. And part of her couldn't help but suspect that this was the intended effect.

Chapter Two

Rain spattered the window. Val watched the drops from her bed as they coursed slowly down the glass, keeping her eye on two in particular — waiting to see which would win the race. She was betting on the one on the left. There were more droplets in its path, more opportunities to gain momentum and pick up speed.

"Val, are you — " Mrs. Kimble's words cut off as she poked her head into her daughter's bedroom and saw her lying partially off her bed while staring at the window upside-down. "What on earth are you doing?"

Val didn't take her eyes from the window. "Watching the rain."

Mrs. Kimble laughed, or started to, but she turned it into a cough. She said sternly, "Well you can't stay in bed all day. Go do something productive. Read. Watch TV. Call Lisa."

"Watching TV is productive? Since when?"

"Valerian Marie Kimble, if you do not get out of that bed right this instant I'm going to take away your computer."

Val slid her legs off her pink comforter, throwing a backwards glance at the window. The raindrop on the left had won, she was satisfied. She trailed after her mother, who was headed for the kitchen. "Don't eat anything," Mrs. Kimble warned. "I'm making dinner."

Val made a face at her turned back and snatched a bottle of juice from the fridge and a bag of sunflower seeds, pinching the crinkly bag between her fingertips as she ran back to her room, shutting the door so her mother wouldn't hear the crunching and investigate.

She set the snack on her desk and picked up her cell phone. Call Lisa, her mother had said. Ugh. Lisa's mother probably didn't make her get out of bed; in fact, she probably would have been happy. She was always grounding Lisa for staying out too late or going over her phone plan, which was why Val was calling her house number, and not her cell phone.

Horror of horrors, this meant Mrs. Jeffries picked up the phone. "Hello?"

"Um, hi, Mrs. Jeffries."

"Oh, *Val*, is that you? You're practically *family*, dear. Please, call me *Donna*."

"Is Lisa there?" Val asked, unable to keep the desperation

from her voice. "Could I — "

"Lisa's in the *bathroom*, as usual," Mrs. Jeffries said, "Curling her *hair*. How are you, *Val*? I feel like I haven't spoken to you in *ages*."

That was not an accident. "I guess I've been so busy lately, with track and stuff. Lisa — "

"That's *right*. You're on the *track* team. How is your *mother*, Val?"

"She — "

"You're such a *pleasure* to talk to, Val, such a good *listener*."

Only because talking to Mrs. Jeffries left one with no other choice. *Help*, thought Val.

Salvation came in the form of a shout in the background. "Mom, is that Val?"

"Darling, we're *inside* — use your *indoor* voice. Yes, it's your little friend, *Val*. We were just catching *up*, weren't we, Val?"

Val bristled at being called 'little.'

"Gimmie the phone, Mom. God — give it — you always do this!"

There was the sound of a scuffle and a barely-muffled

argument, and then Lisa's sigh of relief crackling like a burst of static as she finally managed to wrest the phone away.

"Sorry about that," Lisa said breathlessly. "I try to pick up first, but *Mom* beat me to it this time. She seriously needs to get some friends of her own and stop trying to pick off mine."

"I thought she was going to meet up with those army wives she met online."

"Been there, done that, gotten the t-shirt. It didn't work out."

Lisa's father was currently serving in Afghanistan. "Why?" she asked. "You'd think she'd be able to manage to overcome any differences — "

"You'd think so, but no. She made them all hate her. They won't return her calls now."

"How did that happen?"

"She wouldn't tell *me*. All I got out of her was that they were a bunch of gossipy bitches and that she was never going back there again and blah, blah, blah — just like high school."

"That sucks."

"Oh, God. Tell me about it. Knowing her, she probably brought up some icky subject and wouldn't take a hint when one of them started kicking at her leg to shut her up. But whatever, I am so tired of my mom. What's going on with you?"

"I've been reduced to raindrop-racing."

"That's a new low, even for you."

"You can make fun of me for it, or you can help me *do* something about it. Pick one."

"Can't I have both?"

"No."

"Fine. I suppose we can go out."

Val sighed. Good. Now her mother would get off her back.

"Where do you want to go?"

"Where do *you* want to go?" Val asked, "You know I hate deciding."

"We can go to that indie coffee place and flirt with the hot baristas."

"I'm not supposed to eat. The *hausfrau* is making dinner."

"We could go to the used record store and listen to music until they kick us out."

"We did that last weekend. I *like* going there. I don't want to end up blacklisted like they did to James."

"James was throwing CDs at his friends, and only because his older brother gave him one of those Cocaine energy drinks. But that's just fine, Miss Picky-Pants. What do *you* want to do?"

Val groaned inwardly. "Bowling?"

"Maybe if we were both nine, and at somebody's lame-ass birthday party."

"Movie?"

"Nothing good's out."

"Bookstore?"

"Are you kidding? I'm already behind in my readings for honors English. I don't need *more* books."

"Well — " Val thought desperately. This was exactly why she hated making decisions. "Um, they just opened a new Petville in the Derringer Shopping Plaza. Do you want to go there and look around? See if they have any cute baby animals?"

"Oh, all right," said Lisa, "and maybe I'll even pick up some Starbucks, too. Is your mom driving? I don't want to ask mine."

"Hang on." Val set the phone down on the desk. "Hey, Mom?"

"Yes?" Slightly muffled. She was digging in the freezer.

"Can you drive Lisa and me to the Petville at the shopping center?"

Her mother peered out from behind the fridge door. "*Pet*ville? As in a pet store?"

"Just to look, not to buy. And I'll wash my hands really good before eating."

"Really well," Mrs. Kimble corrected automatically. "I suppose. It's my fault for telling you to get out of the house, isn't it? It wouldn't be right to punish you for taking me up on it." She set a bag of frozen vegetables on the speckled granite counter. "Let me just put these in the crock pot."

So, in other words, she'd be another fifteen minutes.

Val needed to change clothes, anyway. She wasn't about to go out in public in her sweatpants — not the ones from her old middle school, anyway. She had standards, in spite of what Lisa liked to think. Speaking of which, she still had her on hold, didn't she?

Val picked up her phone and caught strains of bored

humming. "Lisa? My mom says yes."

"Thank God — get here as soon as you can."

You're welcome, thought Val, as the line went dead.

Val selected a drab green sweater from her closet, and a pair of jeans that were starting to wear out around the knees. Sometimes when she got bored in class, she would pick at the threads until they snapped off in her hand. She slipped her foot into one of her black flats and then went hunting for the other pair, eventually finding it behind the garbage can beneath her desk. How had it gotten *there*? And why did her shoes always manage to scatter themselves?

Just another unsolvable mystery of the universe, she decided. *Like why it takes dumb boys days to respond to Facebook messages even when they are obviously online.* No, he wouldn't fooling anybody, and it was only making him look like a jerk.

Val studied her computer.

Might as well. Mom takes forever, anyway.

And she was curious to see if James had finally responded to her message. The one that she had sent two days ago. It wasn't even like she'd asked him out; she just wanted to know if he'd be down for seeing a movie with her *and* Lisa sometime.

The whole thing had, naturally, been Lisa's idea.

According to Lisa, James had just broken up with his girlfriend of two weeks. The reasons behind the breakup were unclear, though Lisa had heard rumors that the girl had cheated on him with a varsity quarterback.

Apparently, James had also, when asked, said that he thought Val "seemed pretty cool." But while Lisa seemed thrilled by this, Val couldn't bring herself to think of the compliment (if that's what it really was — it seemed more likely that he just couldn't think of anything else to say) particularly heartening, and certainly not the veiled declaration of love Lisa seemed to interpret it as, since Val was pretty sure she'd heard James refer to his math teacher in the exact same way.

His *male* math teacher.

Still, she guessed it was better than if he had simply said, "Val, who?" Now it was, "Oh, that girl from track?"

Track had really helped Val find herself. The girls on the team were so sweet and supportive; it had been hard to stay in her shell when they always dragged her out for post-meet coffees. Plus, running had made her feel empowered. It made her feel *powerful*. She loved that feeling when she was nearing her limits but still managed to press on. It was such a head rush.

She opened the Facebook page, pleased to see some notifications. One was from Rachel and Lindsay, who had sent her an invite to a fundraiser for new track uniforms. Val selected "attending" and scrolled to the waiting message; it wasn't from James, though (*even though he's totally online — I can see you, you jerk*), but someone she didn't know. The name looked fake.

The picture was an off-putting photograph of a man in Victorian garb facing away from the camera. He was wearing a tophat. She made a face. Another one of those cosplaying weirdos? Ever since she'd made the mistake of joining that stupid "Girl Gamers" Facebook group, she'd been getting all kinds of messages from guys — some of them old enough to be her dad. She wondered what this creep wanted.

Valerian —

I've seen you on the field, how savage you can be, blazing like a fire bolt as you race for the finish line. I'm intrigued ... enough that I want to see more. Know more. Know you.

Tell me, why is it that you run? Is it to chase? Or to flee?

I'd give a lot to know.

Oh, dear God. It was from a crazy man — and he knew who she was, what she did, where she ran. That was far worse than if he had been a perfect stranger.

"You about ready, honey?"

Val jumped, flashing her mother a guilty smile. "Yeah." She shut her laptop. *It's probably just a prank. Somebody's trying to mess with me.*

I hope.

■□■□■□■

"Now make sure you call me when you girls are done looking," Val's mother said.

"Yes, Mom."

"Yes, Mrs. Kimble."

"Stay in this general area. I'll pick you up right here where I dropped you off."

"*Yes*, Mom."

Mrs. Kimble eyed the two of them for a moment. "All right. Have fun, girls."

"Your mom is overprotective," Lisa remarked as they walked up to Petville.

"She isn't! She's just concerned."

"Concerned enough to mess herself."

"She was a bit wild when she was my age."

"And she's afraid you're going to pull all the stops? You're practically a saint."

"I am not! I can be wild, too!"

"Yeah, when I think 'Valerian Kimble,' I think, 'Now there's a girl I don't want to mess with' — or at least, that's what I would think if I had a chronic fear of freakishly nice people."

Val punched her in the arm.

"You know, something? If this were a horror movie, you would totally be the murderer," Lisa said, rubbing her arm, "You're too good to be true."

"Good thing this isn't a horror movie then — or is it?" Val gave her the evil eye.

"Very nice. I almost felt a shiver coming on. What is that

smell?"

Val sniffed. Petville smelled exactly how she expected a pet store to smell — dust, animal poop, and cat food. But Lisa wrinkled her nose the moment her Sketchers made contact with the dirty tiles.

"On second thought," said Lisa, "I do feel a shiver coming on. Be right back. Maybe." She shot a dubious look at the aisle of kitty litter nearby. "I'm going to buy my coffee before I lose my appetite."

"Lisa — "

"Go find a puppy to play with. Maybe *it* will be afraid of you."

Val stuck her tongue out at her, but Lisa had already turned around.

Finding a puppy does sound like a good idea, though. I wonder if they have any.

Val came to the aquariums first. There were the ubiquitous bug-eyed goldfish, sometimes as many as twenty to a tank. Across the way were some Siamese fighting fish with fins that looked like the trailing, patterned sleeves kimono. For the caregiving-challenged, there were some aquatic snails. Val tapped one of the bettas' tanks. The fish had been drifting around disinterestedly and looked as if it could use some livening up.

The fish slammed its body against the glass and Val started, and said, "Oh!"

A quiet laugh sounded from somewhere behind her. Val turned just in time to see one of the employees looking away, as if he hadn't been mocking her just now. She narrowed her eyes.

"What's so funny?"

"They're called fighting fish for a reason," he said, smiling as he strolled away.

Jerk.

Val left the fish section — because she wanted to — and soon found herself in the pet toy section. Looking at the pet toys always made her feel a little giddy. She liked to imagine what kinds of toys she'd play with herself if she were an animal. She suspected this made her a freak but there was no denying that she was a fuzzy mouse-chaser at heart. She made the bell on one jingle; it was filled with catnip.

Watching Lisa play with her cat, Duchess, had always

filled Val with jealousy. She loved cats. She loved how human they were, how each one had its own personality and its own likes and dislikes. Duchess held her tail up high, curled like a question mark, when she was curious; when she was disdainful, her snubs were as pointed as a cheerleader sticking up her nose.

Dogs were like that, too. You could tell just by looking at a dog on its leash whether it was a nice dog or a mean dog. The nice ones had gentle faces and kind eyes, their tongues hanging out of their mouths in a goofy, eager-to-please grin. The mean ones, with their narrowed eyes and bared teeth, just looked, well, mean.

It was harder to tell with humans, which was what made them so distinct from other animals. Sometimes the nice ones could look mean, and sometimes the mean ones could look nice. And sometimes it was impossible to tell at all. *At least with animals you know where you stand,* Val thought, frowning and crossing her arms as she walked out of the toy aisle.

In the back of the store was a plastic play structure surrounded by glass. Inside were a dozen kittens colored orange and black like tigers. Three of them were engaged in rough-and-tumble play, the end result being a squirming pile of tails and paws and ears. Their high-pitched mews made Val's heart melt instantly.

She knelt down to read the placard on the side of the pen. *Toyger kittens: A relatively new crossbreed, so named for their distinctive facial and bodily characteristics that make them resemble toy tigers. Toygers are energetic, curious, friendly, and, despite their fierce appearance, quite tame—not at all like their wild cousins!*

Her eyes widened. Good lord. They were $600 each.

Cute, though. Heck, if she had the money, she'd probably buy one. They were precious. One of the toygers wandered over to where she was examining the sign and mewed at her. Grinning, Val raised her finger to the level of its nose and watched its bright blue eyes track the motion.

Its white-tipped paws scrabbled at the glass, and she laughed out loud at its puzzled expression. It seemed bewildered by the peculiar force-field keeping it from interacting in greater depth with its prey.

"Hey, cutie. You are a cutie, aren't you? Oh, you want my finger?"

Scratch, scratch, scratch.

"You do, don't you! Wheeeee, look at the finger go! You can't get me!"

Scratch, scratch.

"Don't give up. Look! Here I come again!"

The kitten headbutted the glass, and one of its ears twitched. It shot her an accusatory look.

She laughed again. "Silly."

"Would you like to see one?"

She looked up from the kitten she was playing with. It was the employee again. The one who had laughed at her back at the fish tanks. His face was quite serious now, though.

With his strikingly pale eyes, and stubbled chin, he looked every bit as wild as the toyger, but a good deal less friendly.

Had he heard her talking in that stupid voice? Had he been watching her?

The thought filled her with horror.

Val got to her feet with poise, noting he was quite a bit taller than she was. Not a big deal, but something she noticed nonetheless, being of above-average height herself. "I'm not, um, buying." She brushed her hands over her jeans. "I was just looking."

The kittens were so expensive; maybe they were high-strung. She was going to get kicked out, wasn't she?

The boy's lips quirked. "I didn't ask if you were buying. I asked if you wanted to see one. Hold one."

"I couldn't …." But her tone said differently.

And before she could muster up the strength for a proper refusal, he had unlocked the door and picked up her kitten by the scruff of its neck, depositing it neatly into her hands. The kitten looked her with large eyes; she could feel it trembling from the fear and excitement of its journey outside the pen.

"Oh," she sighed, and ran her fingertips over its silky fur. "So soft."

"Quite."

"How old are they?"

With her eyes on the kitten, she didn't notice the way he looked her up and down, or how his eyes climbed upward from her flats and lingered. "A few weeks, I imagine."

"Such a sweet baby." She scratched under its chin. Soon her palm was vibrating with purrs. "They're so cute."

"They are that. But not nearly as impressive as the

genuine article."

His voice was strange enough to make Val look up, and she caught him looking at the little kitten with something that was almost … distaste. But surely not. She wondered if she had imagined that cold sneer; his expression was once again congenial as he met her eyes.

"In any case, he certainly seems to have taken to you."

"It's a boy?"

"You don't know how to tell?"

Val's face flushed. "I — I didn't check."

"I rather think he wants to go home with you."

As if in agreement, the kitten licked her hand with its small rough tongue, rubbing its face against her fingers for more petting.

"Story of my life," she said, steadying the kitten with her other hand as it tried to spill over her fingers. "Animals love me, but I'm not allowed any pets." Her laugh subsided into a small gasp when the kitten, growing restless, decided to go after her charm bracelet. Small beads of blood welled up as she pried its small claws and fangs out of her wrist.

"I think it's time to put him back." She handed the toyger

off to the boy, who put him into the pen a touch roughly.

"Their claws are sharp." She stared down at her wrist, squeezing the wound. "Jesus. *Ow*."

"You sound surprised. They're killers in miniature."

The thought of a killer kitten nearly made her laugh, and she would have if the boy weren't so unsettling. "Do you happen to have any bandages?"

"Yes, in the back. Some antibiotic, too, I think." He glanced at her hand. "Shall I get both? I'm not sure how clean that pen is — it might get infected."

"If you don't mind," she said, feeling shy.

"Go ahead and sit down. I'll see what we have."

She plopped down on the edge of the bench he'd indicated, watching the frolicking kittens and marveling that something so small and seemingly helpless could cause so much pain — even by accident.

Killers in miniature.

"Give me your wrist." Val started, looking up at him. He was back with bandages and some disinfectants. "Your wrist," he repeated.

"Oh," she said, and proffered the hand.

He studied the wounds, his eyes dispassionate, even clinical, although his grip, as he wrapped his fingers around her wrist, was just a little too firm to be comfortable. "Not too deep," he remarked as his fingertips lightly grazed the edges of the wounds. "That's good. It'll heal faster."

"You'll get blood on you," Val warned.

"Blood washes off." He smoothed the bandage over her skin. "You look familiar."

"I do?"

"Your hair is very distinctive."

She clutched one of the offending copper locks. "Who are you?"

He held his finger to his lips. "You'll figure it out."

The doors opened and they both turned as Lisa's head bobbed into appearance. She was wielding a large sugary confection that resembled a milkshake more than a coffee. With the hand the boy wasn't still holding onto, Val waved.

Lisa's head pivoted, and her eyes narrowed. "What happened to you?" she demanded, her tone harsh.

"I got mauled by a kitten."

"They have kittens?" Her expression thawed a little when

she glanced at the pen. "Oh my God. What breed are they?"

"Toygers," the boy said. To Val, he said, "I'm done."

Lisa gave Val a sharp look. She turned to the boy and when she spoke, the object of her sudden ire was immediately clear. "What the hell is a toyger?"

"A cat bred to look like a tiger."

"Thanks for clearing that up. Is the sarcasm extra?"

"Stating the obvious can be very trying," the boy replied.

"Excuse me?" Lisa's voice took on a dangerous quality.

"You heard me."

"I should report you to your supervisor. Is this how you treat all your customers?"

Val felt unease nip at her stomach. "Lisa …." Lisa waved her off. The boy merely laughed.

"Oh, you think that's funny? Why don't you go write another hate list?"

His laughter subsided into a quiet, "Perhaps I will."

"Let me guess. I'll at the top."

"You would be … but from what I hear, you prefer to be on the bottom."

Lisa flinched as if he'd slapped her. "Fuck you."

He raised an eyebrow at Val as if to say *See?*

Val tried again, "Lisa …"

Lisa wasn't having it. "Fuck off. I'm not going to argue — I'm not going to argue semantics with *assholes*. Come on, Val, we're leaving."

"But — "

Lisa had a good hold on her wrist and dragged her away before Val could even finish her protest. Val glanced back, to see the boy still watching her, lowering his hand from his face. The hand he'd used to bandage her wrist. Was he …? No. That was insane. There was no way he'd licked her blood from his hand. She was crazy for even thinking it.

Wasn't she?

Stupid. People don't drink blood.

"What the hell are you doing?" Lisa said, barely waiting until they were outside the automatic doors. "I leave you alone for fifteen minutes and you immediately decide to embark on an expedition of social suicide?"

Val yanked her wrist out of Lisa's grip. She felt a little dizzy. Something to chalk up to the blood loss, maybe. She rubbed at her hand and said, "What are you snapping about?"

"I'm snapping about you and Gavin Mecozzi."

"Who's that?"

"Who else?"

"Him?" She tilted her head towards Petville.

"The one who practically just called me a slut to my face? The one you were getting all chummy with? Yeah, that's the one. Good job, Val. Gold star. You win the multiple choice."

"We were not getting chummy! Why are you mad at me? I didn't know. I've never even heard of him."

"Well, obviously." Lisa rolled her eyes, but to Val's relief, her anger was beginning to dissipate. "People only tell you nice things. There's nothing nice to say about Gavin. He's a freak. He's weird, and his family is crazy. End of story."

Val was silent.

Lisa sighed. "Look. I know how you get around sad saps, but he's no socially awkward loser. There's a reason he's not popular and it isn't because he's not attractive, or nonathletic. He scares people."

"He doesn't scare me." But even as she said it, Val knew it was a lie.

"He should," Lisa said bluntly. "And if he doesn't — well,

there's something wrong with you."

Fearscape by Nenia Campbell

Chapter Three

Gavin Mecozzi.

About 1,001 results (0.14 seconds).

Conflicting emotions welled up inside Val as she stared at the Google page. Curiosity warred with the niggling suspicion that she should probably leave well enough alone. This didn't make her a creeper, did it? She was pretty sure it did.

Lisa had a lot of nerve telling her who to stay away from, especially after that lecture about how she was "too good." Hadn't the implication been that she needed a bad influence?

Val eyed the page again. 1,001 results was a lot. She wasn't sure how she was going to get through all of them, or even half of them. Was this really what stalkers did in their free time? *They must have a lot of free time.*

"Val, I'm dropping you off at school in forty minutes. Will you be ready?"

"*Yes*, Mom!"

She heard her mother utter something sarcastic as she walked away. Something about ingratitude.

Could people find out if you had been Google-searching them? She would absolutely die if Gavin found out she had been stalking him. Or if Lisa found out.

No, wait, she didn't care about that. Screw Lisa.

Since Val was not about to go through 1,001 web pages, she repeated the search by putting his name into quotes this time. The results narrowed down to a doable 230 — and she *knew* some of those highlighted names had to be her Gavin, because they were clearly local. Petville's website turned up, as did that of DHS, something called FIDE, and a genealogy site.

She was definitely checking the latter out, but what on earth was FIDE? A company? She opened another tab and started a third search. Fédération Internationale des Échecs.

The World Chess Federation.

She scanned the page and learned from the site's succinct summary that the group had been founded in Paris, and the catchy acronym of the French name had stuck). Gavin, when she searched for him, was listed as holding the title of "master" with a ranking of 2300.

His opponents said of him, "he weaves his traps as neatly and intricately as a spider spins its web — beautifully done, and just as lethal," "a brutal force of nature, terrible, wondrous, and completely unstoppable," and "truly, his games made for some of the most memorable in my experience."

Gavin seemed to have given that up, though, because he was listed as inactive. Val wondered why he'd quit. She looked up his rating because "master" sounded impressive and the only comparison she could come up with were the numerical rankings of SAT scores. She was amazed to see that his rating grouped him with some of the best players in the entire *world*.

That stunned her into thoughtful contemplation for several seconds.

Val couldn't imagine what it would be like to be that good at something, let alone something as intellectual and sophisticated and exotic as chess. Her father played, but he wasn't very good. He'd tried to teach her a handful of times when she was young, but Val had been dismissive of the dull-colored pieces with their stunning lack of decoration and had only wanted to play Candy Land.

I wonder if I'd be a master right now if I had let Dad teach me.

Val closed the FIDE tab and opened up the genealogy website. Anna Mecozzi was the first name that leaped out at her, with lines trailing from her name like spider silk. Val's eyes followed the lines, which widened with comprehension as she reached their end.

She was Gavin's mother.

Gavin's name was the first name listed, but his father's was conspicuously absent. Did that meant he didn't know who his father was? Maybe he was adopted. That wasn't so depressing.

But they do something special to the lines when you're adopted, I can't remember what ....

Val stared at the chart. God, he had a lot of siblings. Anna-Maria, Luca, Leona, Nicola, Dorian, Adelaide, Celesta. She wondered if he was Catholic. Italians were Catholic, weren't they? Was he Italian? His name certainly was, and he had the same dark, brooding looks of the Italian actors popularized in films.

As she read more, she learned that he was, indeed, Italian. He was the first and only child his mother had given birth to on her native Lombardian soil before immigrating and then living as an expatriate on the Eastern seaboard.

Anna Mecozzi was an ex-thespian and appeared to collect

men the way other women collected stamps or coins. Val experienced quite a shock when she glimpsed a picture. The woman was gorgeous — blonde and petite, with high cheekbones and surprisingly thin lips. She looked nothing like her tall, swarthy son.

Except for her eyes. They had the same cold, colorless eyes.

Val closed the genealogy site and clicked to see what the school had to say about him.

Gavin had been touted as an expert in the archery club. There was a stunning picture of him on the school's website, wearing a muscle shirt and sweatpants, holding a bow with an arrow poised and ready on the taut string taking aim at the photographer.

Val wondered who had taken that photograph of him. His intense, focused expression said both that he wouldn't think twice about shooting whomever lay behind the lens, and that he wasn't going to miss if he did.

Apparently, he'd also dabbled on the men's swim team as a freshman, but had quit before the season was through, so while his name was listed among those assembled, he, himself, wasn't. She felt her face grow hot as she realized that she was a little disappointed.

He didn't seem crazy, though. Weird, yes. Interesting, yes. Dangerous, definitely.

Crazy, no.

She clicked back to the archery photo. *I wonder if he's still that buff.* Beneath the clinging gray fabric, she thought she could make out the slight contour of his abs. He had nice shoulders, too, muscular — from swimming, she supposed — and his arms looked strong. As if he'd be able to pick up a girl her size without much difficulty ….

"Val, ten minute warning!"

She nearly fell over herself changing the screen back to Facebook. "I'm coming, Mom! Jeez."

With a last look at her empty message box, she closed her laptop and sighed. Look at her, acting like a drooling idiot over someone she would, in all likelihood, never see again.

(You'll figure it out.)

Right?

"Val, are you ready?"

"Yes."

Fearscape by Nenia Campbell

■□■□■□■

Val's day at Derringer High School passed uneventfully.

In Art, they were beginning to study the human form in preparation for the life drawing they would begin for the next few weeks. Giggles abounded when Ms. Wilcox informed them that despite the fact life drawing classes generally involved naked models, there would be no nudes.

Val squirmed at the thought, relieved she would be spared such a gross indignity.

James was sitting with his jock friends, and he was one of the people laughing the hardest. Val stared down at her blank piece of paper and wondered again why Lisa was so convinced that the two of them had anything in common. She was beginning to suspect Lisa knew no such thing, and the fact that James was cute was supposed to be enough.

Ms. Wilcox eyed her students with fond disapproval. "Now that you've gotten that out of your system, I expect total silence while you sketch. Total," she said, switching off the radio, "Silence."

The back of Val's neck prickled as the room was plunged into a hush broken only by the sound of scribbling pens and pencils, and whispered giggles. She had the same creepy feeling she'd gotten on the track field, and then again in the girls' locker room.

Her fingers closed around her pencil as if it were a weapon. She tried to think about what she wanted to draw, but her thoughts were occluded by swirls of uneasiness mired in irritation. For some reason, she thought of those fierce-looking little kittens from Petville. They had been so beautiful, what with their detailed markings and large blue eyes. Maybe should draw them. And then her hand was moving almost before she'd even completed the thought, describing wispy tufts of baby-soft fur, velvet whiskers, liquid eyes.

"Nice use of detail, Val," Ms. Wilcox said, in passing.

Val smiled in response, using the tip of her finger to smudge and blend the stripes. "I love animals," she said, more to herself than her teacher.

It was the one bright spot in her day.

After Art was English, which Val hated. Mrs. Vasquez brandished works of literature the way other people, in crueler times, surely must have wielded pitchforks and spears. Before the more standard *Romeo and Juliet*, Val's teacher had gotten them started on *Titus Andronicus*, which was absolutely awful. Murder and rape and torture — but everyone else in the class was pretty enthusiastic about it, which meant Val had to pretend to like it, too, so they wouldn't make fun of her the way they did the one Mormon girl in the class.

Emily Abernathy, the Mormon, was on a customized lesson plan since her religion precluded many of the books and movies Mrs. Vasquez had them watch in class, including the 1960s movie with the infamous flash of boob. Many of the boys were looking forward to that movie. *James included, probably,* thought Val, leaning on the heel of her hand with annoyance.

"We'll also be watching the movie, *Titus*," Mrs. Vasquez was saying, "So I'll be passing out permission slips. If you don't turn them in by the end of the week, you can't watch the movie."

Oh, really? Val immediately resolved to lose hers. These things happened, after all, and an imposed study session in the library under the hawkish eyes of crabby old Ms. Banner was far more appealing than watching people get chopped up and baked into pies. Just the thought made Val want to throw up.

Emily looked equally discomfited. She caught Val's look of horror and gave her a shy, strained smile of camaraderie.

Mrs. Vasquez looked at Val, then at Emily, and said, "If you don't watch the movie" — *how could she possibly know what I was thinking?* " — I'll be expecting a five-page analysis of your thoughts on *Titus Andronicus*, along with detailed examples and quotes from the play."

Fudge, thought Val, and from Emily's face, it was clear she was thinking the same thing. *I hate English.*

She ended the day with Health, which wasn't much better. Some poor college girl had been recruited to tell her story about alcohol poisoning after a party gone wrong. *It sounds like something out of one of those Lifetime movies Mrs. Jeffries watches*, Val thought, as the girl talked about waking up with her head in a toilet, and how she had panicked when she started puking blood. Val wanted to puke herself.

The bell cut the girl off just as she started talking about her enlarged pancreas and unpleasant emergency visit to the hospital. *Thank God*, thought Val. *Saved by the bell.*

"How was school?" Mrs. Kimble asked.

Val yanked open the door and plunked herself into the passenger seat. "Gross."

"Gross?"

"People vomiting blood and getting chopped up."

"That must have been an interesting lesson."

"It wasn't."

"Well, I have some errands to run. Do you want to come with me, or shall I drop you off at home?"

Val started to say "home" and paused. "Could I go to Petville?"

"Val, I've told you — "

"Not to buy. It's just — they have these baby kittens. They're the cutest things ever, Mom, I've never seen anything like them before. They're a new breed — I'm drawing them for Art."

"This is a school thing?"

Val nodded. That cinched it.

"Oh, all right. How long do you think you'll be?"

"I have my phone," said Val. "You can call me when it's time to pick me up. And then I'll come out to the parking lot and wait."

"You certainly have this planned out."

Val colored. "Mom! God, not everything's a conspiracy, you know."

"It is when you're blushing," her mother said, which only caused the flush to deepen. "What on earth are you planning?"

"My art project," Val mumbled, swinging herself out of the car door when her mother pulled into the shopping center. "I'll call you when I'm done."

Stupid, nosy mothers.

The automatic doors slid open with a whir as she walked towards the store. Val's chest tightened, and she tightened her grip on the strap of her backpack.

The strange boy was glaringly absent — not that she was looking. In his place was a heavyset man in a blue apron her eyed her with undisguised suspicion, staring at the sketchpad under her arm. Val looked around nervously before approaching the man and explaining what she wanted.

"I just want to draw them," she said, shrinking under his gaze, "I won't touch or bother them or anything like that. It's for, um, school."

Fearscape by Nenia Campbell

The man grunted something like reluctant quiescence before going off to harangue some middle schoolers Val recognized from last year, when she was in eighth grade, for pestering the beta fish and laughing as they attacked the glass.

Val shook her head, hoping she hadn't been that annoying at twelve, and sat cross-legged in front of the kitten pen, wincing a little at the grimy dustiness of the floor. A few of the kittens crawled over to the wall to stare at her and mew. Val was flooded with the urge to coo over them, but the image of the stern-faced store manager dampened that impulse.

Slowly, conscious of the manager's menacing presence, Val began to sketch. At first she used grids to try and map the proportions of the kittens' faces. She realized immediately that she had made their foreheads much too small and their cheeks much too fat in her preliminary sketch.

As she sat erasing, she was aware of a shadow crossing her pad. She looked up, startled, to see the fat man hovering over her. "Are you an artist?"

"I guess," said Val, stiffening a little as she looked back at her paper.

"Hmm." The man grunted again. "That's quite good."

"Thank you." She could feel her cheeks getting warm. She wished he would go away.

"There's a boy works here — he's an artist, too."

At that, Val looked up. "Really? How old is he?"

"Old enough to know better, young enough to worry about."

Now what on earth did that mean? Val wanted to ask him more, but the man had grown tired of the subject and walked off towards the rows of bird cages, shaking his head and muttering as he resumed tailing the rowdy group of preteens through the store.

That was weird.

Val finished her sketches, brushing the man's strange words off like the dust from the floor, and checked her phone for new messages. No calls from her mother, which meant she was probably still shopping. Instead of calling for early pickup, Val walked over to the Starbucks two stores down to get herself a drink while she waited.

The coffee shop was crowded because of the grocery stores nearby. Val waited in line, flipping through her sketchbook to study her drawings, and also secretly hoping that someone walking by might comment, when she was suddenly compelled to look up.

There, sitting at one of the tables by the window with a half-drunk espresso, was the boy from Petville. Staring — at her.

(There's a boy works here. He's an artist, too.)

I wonder if he's the artist.

But such a coincidence seemed too great. There had to be dozens of people his age — *our age* — working there. The artist could have been anyone, a college student, maybe.

Funny, though, her running into him here.

Don't be stupid. He's probably on break or something.

"What can I get for you today?" the barista asked.

"An iced hazelnut latte, please."

"That'll be three dollars and fifty cents."

Val came up with exactly two-fifty. The barista fixed her with an annoyed look, glancing over Val's shoulder at the long line building up behind her. Val's face flushed. *Where is that other dollar? I know I had more money in here.*

"Miss? You still owe me a dollar. People are waiting."

"I know. Um." Val wished the floor would just open up

and swallow her whole. "I don't think — "

"I'll take care of it," said a deep, amused voice.

Val looked up in shock. Gavin had left both his table and his drink unattended, and was handing the barista a crumpled dollar. She couldn't believe what she was seeing. It was like something out of a book. She didn't know this boy or anything about him, really, and yet here he was, stepping in to her rescue like a hero from a harlequin romance.

Except he's not the hero, she reminded herself. Lisa had made that painfully clear.

"Wait," she said, "You don't have to — "

"It's fine," he said smoothly, slipping his wallet back into his pocket.

Val crossed to the other side of the counter, blinking back tears. She wasn't sure why she was so upset, but she was. That had been *so* embarrassing — and then he had just paid for her, out of the blue. Who did that? Not that she wasn't grateful, because she was, but she was nervous, and her nervousness was intensified by the sheer force of her gratitude. It threatened to bowl her over as he sauntered over to where she stood, pointedly not looking at him.

Indebted, that was the word for her feelings. She felt indebted.

"You're welcome," he prompted.

"Thank you."

"Is that all you have to say to me?"

What else was she supposed to say?

When the barista called out her name, mispronouncing it as "Valerie" the way everyone did, he took her drink, and Val was forced to chase after him, all the way back to his table. She reached for the cup and he shook his head, sliding it out of reach so that she would be forced to slide in beside him to reclaim it. At her hesitation, he said, "I don't bite."

Resigned, she plopped into the booth and sat away from him as far as possible.

He was wearing a black and white checked shirt beneath a black V-necked sweater, and one of those newsboy caps all the hipsters wore. He didn't look like a hipster, though, not even with those glasses. He didn't look quite like anything she had ever seen before.

He cleared his throat, and she realized with no small amount of embarrassment that she'd been caught staring. "Are you always this reticent?"

"You were rude to my friend," she said in response.

"Mm, that's right. You're the girl from a few days ago," he mused. "Valerian — Val."

Val stiffened. "You — you remember my name?" *Now that's a first.*

He smiled at his espresso as he took a sip. "I remember more than that."

"She told me I should stay away from you."

"I figured," he said pleasantly. "That's why I used a lure. How's the wrist?"

"It's healed," Val said, "What lure? What are you talking about?"

"Making you come to me. With this." He tapped his cup.

Val's frown deepened. "You shouldn't be so dismissive. I think you hurt Lisa's feelings."

"What a pity." He set down his mug and laced his fingers together. "She'll get over it."

"Why are you acting like this?"

Gavin chuckled, shaking his head. "How else should I act?"

"Nice."

"I'm not nice."

"Then why did you do that?"

He arched an eyebrow. "What, bandage your wrist?"

"Yes, that. And buy my drink. You don't know me." She winced — that sounded prudish and pedantic even to her own ears — but she didn't backpedal towards an apology. She wanted to know the answer. "Why would you help me?"

"Maybe I'd like to," he said, taking another sip of coffee. He paused. "Know you, that is."

"You can't have possibly decided that already."

"You're in my art class, Val. I've seen your work. It's very interesting."

Val swallowed hard. "First period?"

He nodded.

"With Ms. Wilcox?" At his nod, she said, "No way, I would have noticed — "

"I sit in the back. I'm usually working. I'm the TA for that class, so I arrive quite early."

"Oh," said Val. "Then you're the one who — who draws all the animals. Like the tiger, and the wolf — "

"Yes."

"They're so good."

He half-smiled. "Thank you."

"No, I mean — *really* good. How do you make them so real?"

"How do you get on so well with animals?"

The question caught her off-guard. "I — I don't."

"That's not what I've heard. You're getting quite the reputation. You, and your feline friends."

"Lisa," Val muttered.

"That, and the fact that the local animal shelters can't wait to get their hands on you."

"It's really not that big of a deal."

"Oh? Do tell."

"I just, um, think of them as little people."

"Well, I suppose I think of myself as a big animal. Very apropos, isn't it?" He smiled, then, and when it came it was more than a little suggestive. Val averted her eyes.

"Don't make fun of me."

"Oh." She felt his fingers brush against her cheek and the overly familiar gesture made her jump. "I'm not making fun of you."

What are you doing, then?

Her phone bleeped, nipping the thought in the bud. Gavin dropped his hand from her face and it was as if a dark spell had been lifted, restoring both mobility and will. "I've got to go," she blurted, and she grabbed her drink from him and walked quickly away, aware of his eyes burning into her back. As she'd made her departure, she had half-expected him to grab her.

To not let her go.

And perhaps the curse hadn't been lifted after all, because a small but significant part of her wouldn't have minded if he had. *What's happening to me?*

Chapter Four

Val kept her eyes peeled in Art to see if Gavin really was in her class as he'd claimed.

It took her longer than she would have guessed to locate him. For such a tall boy, he camouflaged himself with remarkable ease. A black t-shirt and dark jeans rendered him nearly invisible in a school where 90% of the population wore that color as a fashion statement.

Locate him she did, though, and she took advantage of his distraction with his charcoals to study him raptly. He was sitting in the back, which didn't surprise her at all. He was a total mess, which did. At Petville, he struck her as rather fastidious (despite his obvious indifference to blood), but now his hands were smeared gray with the charcoals he was using to sketch. As she watched he adjusted his glasses, leaving smudges of charcoal on his face, as well.

Val found herself with the wild urge to giggle and looked down at her own work in progress before said laugh could manifest itself. Stupid. If he didn't think she was an idiot already, obnoxious laughter and snorts were a surefire way to swing him in that direction.

Fearscape by Nenia Campbell

He probably thought her an utter child.

Her expression sobered as she studied what little advancement she had made on her drawing. She had decided to sketch the kittens from the pet store — and then, later, paint them — but she was having trouble getting their expressions just right. Their eyes looked too human.

Serious now, she tilted her head this way and that to study the painting from new angles. *I suppose I could say it's intentional. That it's — what's the word? — anthropomorphic.*

But she would know, and the minor flaw would bother her until she got it right.

A cold, wet sensation tickled her skin as she shifted her position. The paintbrush was still in her bunched fingers, forgotten until now. She'd been resting her cheek against paint for God knew how long. Val stood up, holding her hands gingerly in front of her, and rinsed herself off in the trough-like sink built into the far wall nearest to the door.

The orange color dripped from her palms and spiraled down the drain, reminding her disconcertingly of blood. Specifically, from the iconic shower scene in *Psycho*. She shook her hands over the basin and tore off a paper towel from the nearby roll. She turned and came close to crashing right into James Lewis.

"Sup?" he said. "You've got paint on your nose."

"Great." She mopped at her face with the damp paper towel. "Did I get it off?"

"Yeah, you're fine now. Oh, by the way — I got your Facebook message."

Val poked a hole through the paper towel. "Did you?"

"Uh-huh. Sorry. I didn't get a chance to respond until this morning and then I had to hightail it to class. I've been busy. Football, you know."

Where Gavin was dark, James was fair. He had auburn hair, about two shades darker and browner than hers and tinged with wires of gold highlights. His eyes were a charming sea foam green and he had a crooked smile that could break a heart.

He was smiling that smile now. The "aww shucks" edition of it, which had gotten him out of trouble successfully, and on more than one occasion too. It might have even worked on Val if that wasn't such a blatant lie. Val was torn between amusement and annoyance. Lies usually went right over her head, blatant or no. She didn't often get the opportunity to call people out on their BS.

But pointing out James's lie wouldn't do her any good. It would only make her look like a desperate stalker, creeping his profile to see if he was online. Make that an extremely possessive stalker. Lisa had told her many times that boys didn't like possessive girls — which was stupid, considering how possessive boys acted.

Val remembered her own stalker, and her stomach tied up in knots of dread. "It's okay," she muttered.

But it wasn't, not really.

James's smile brightened. "Good. I'm glad. Because, you know, I felt pretty bad about that."

I bet you did.

"I'm still down for a movie, though, if you and Lisa are."

Val said nothing, so he pressed on.

"What movie were you guys thinking about? There's a cool action one — "

There was that word "cool" again. What had possessed Lisa to think that this was going to work? James didn't even see her. She could tell. Not as a girl, anyway. Boys didn't look at girls they liked like that.

He obviously doesn't care about anyone but himself....

" — great rating on Rotten Tomatoes — "

A clatter in the back gave her a polite excuse to divert her attention from James's rambling monologue. Gavin was missing from his seat, and his tablemate was staring at the floor. Val's brow furrowed. She could see his hair peeking over the desktop. *What could he possibly be doing?*

" — not a big fan of chick-flicks, but I'd be willing to see — "

He must have dropped something, she decided.

" — good dramatic comedy — "

Oh, he's coming over here!

" — and some horror, if you're into that — " Even James, self-absorbed though he was, noticed his audience's reactions weren't on par with his standards of what constituted raptness. He glanced over to see what had held her attention, and his lip curled. Something Val registered with annoyance.

Ignoring the two of them with a nonchalance that surely had to have been practiced in front of a mirror, Gavin threw away his broken charcoal pencil, now snapped into two distinct pieces. He washed the black from his hands, and his face, and then reached past her to get a paper towel, accidentally brushing her side. She looked up at him and thought she saw him wink.

"So *anyway*, do any of those sound good to you? Lisa says she doesn't care."

Val wadded up her own piece of paper towel, which she had been twisting and knotting in her hands this entire time, and lobbed it into the bin. "I'm not sure."

"Playing hard to get?"

"No. Actually busy. I'm on the track team, you know," she added, unconsciously mocking his earlier tone. At his blank look, she added, "You do know I'm on the track team, right?"

"Uh, yeah. I think I've seen you in uniform before. You wear it on game days, right?

Wearing a sports bra and spandex shorts to school? *Game days?* For heaven's sake. "No, I don't wear it to school. And we don't have game days. I'm not a cheerleader." Val was tired of feeding him hints. "I'm wearing it in my *profile* picture. On Facebook."

Which you would know if you had actually looked at my profile, you liar.

James had the grace to flush. "Ah."

Val eyed him. "You didn't even read my message, did you?"

"I read the email notification on my phone. Same thing."

No, it isn't. She sighed. "I don't think this is going to work."

"Hey," he said, a touch defensively. "There's no need to get all uptight. So track's not my thing."

"This isn't about track." A hot spike of annoyance bored through her, that he could be so stupid. It made her bold. Bold enough to say, "I don't think you understand what I meant. Lisa — our Lisa — was trying to set us up."

The genuine surprise on his face hurt more than if he'd insulted her, point-blank. "What, like on a date?"

"Yes. Like a date."

"Jesus."

"It's not important."

James shook his head. "I didn't think — "

"Really. Don't even worry about it." Feeling suddenly as if she might cry, Val started to walk past him and back towards her seat but James grabbed her arm.

"Hey, wait. I'm sorry."

Val tugged away — but gently. "It doesn't matter."

I don't care, anyway.

She did, though. That was the problem. She did.

Val raked her now-clean fingers through her hair, staring at the unfinished picture of the kittens. She reached for the thinnest of the paintbrushes to go to work on the detailed markings of their striped fur, and her wrist brushed against a balled-up paper set incongruously before the old tin can which held the brushes. *What's this?* She picked it up. *I didn't leave this here.*

She uncrumpled the paper, revealing black, penciled writing done in charcoal.

I think you're exquisite.

Val's heart skipped a beat. *Exquisite? Me?* She looked up and caught Gavin staring at her, his chin resting on the back of his hand as he regarded her through inscrutable, hooded eyes. She pointed to the note and he inclined his head, a small smile curving his lips.

(Maybe I'd like to — know you, that is.)

Val swallowed.

Oh, wow. She thought, *I see.*

■□■□■□■

It was a strangely giddy mood Val found herself in as she walked through the crowded cafeteria to sit at her and her friends' usual table. Rachel and Lindsay were already there. Their Biology teacher was actually pretty cool and always let his class out a few minutes early if their lab stations were neat, which meant they were always first in line for the hot lunches.

Even though brown-bag lunches were so junior high, Mrs. Kimble still insisted upon packing Val's. As Val unpacked her fifth peanut butter and banana sandwich that week, she eyed her friends' grease-laden pizzas and thought the hot lunches might be worth the indigestion.

"Is that friend of yours joining today?" asked Rachel, mouth full. "Whassername?"

"Lisa?"

"I prefer Whassername."

"She should be," said Val. "*Lisa* doesn't have her phone, so I don't know. I can't text her."

"Oh, no," Rachel said, adopting an expression of mock-horror. "Princess lost her phone?"

"Lisa isn't that bad," Val said automatically, wondering even as she said it whether it was true.

"Maybe."

"No maybe," Rachel said. "I'm never going to forget what she said to us."

"What are you — oh, calling us a 'cute couple'?"

"What?" Val said, looking from one to the other, not quite sure if they were serious. "When did this happen? You never told me that Lisa thought you were — "

"Lesbians?" Lindsay supplied, at the same time Rachel said, "Dykes?"

Lindsay glared at her. "Rachel, that's offensive!"

"We both know that's what Miss *Thing* was really thinking."

"I'm sure Lisa didn't mean anything bad by it," Val said uncomfortably.

"She asked me if I listened to *Indigo Girls*."

"And she asked *me* if I played lacrosse."

"You did play lacrosse," Rachel pointed out.

"Yeah, but she didn't know that. She just assumed."

Rachel nodded. "And she asked both of us if we had a Tegan and Sara thing going on."

Oh dear god, thought Val, at the same time that a tray slammed noisily against the fake wood surface of the table. "How do you guys always get here so fast? That line is so gay, no offense."

Lindsay's eyebrow arched so high it nearly disappeared into her hairline. Rachel looked like whether she couldn't decide whether to laugh her head off, or toss back an insult of her own. To Val's relief she settled for a snort of disdain and took a big bite out of her pizza.

Lisa eyed her for a moment, then turned to Val. "So James told me that you're mad at him?"

"I wouldn't say mad. More like annoyed."

Val explained the situation that had transpired in the art room, making an effort to meet the eyes of all three girls in turn. "I guess it's all for the best," she finished. "I mean, he looked surprised."

"What a jerk," said Lindsay. "He's so not even worth your time."

Lisa gave her an evil look. "I'll speak to him, Val. I'm sure he didn't mean it that way."

"I think he did. 'Do you wear your uniform to school on game days?' Come on. Anyway, I'd rather skip the whole he-said she-said deal. Too much gets lost in translation."

"Amen," said Rachel.

"Boys," Lindsay agreed, nodding. "What *doesn't* get lost in translation?"

"Things with the letter X in front of them," Rachel posited. "Like X-Box. And X-rated movies."

"In that case, I'm sure they'd be thrilled if we did wear our uniforms to meet days."

"And be ogled at like we're cheerleaders? No, thanks." Lisa's evil stare got eviller. She was a cheerleader. As if just realizing this, Rachel's eyes widened and she looked at Lisa and said, innocently, "Oh. No offense."

"What about that other guy, Val? The one you were telling us about earlier? The older one?"

"Yes, the one who called you *exquisite*." Rachel batted her eyelashes.

"What older one?" Lisa demanded. "Why didn't I — " she broke off, now focusing her evil stare on Val. "Oh, no. You didn't."

"It's not like that," Val stammered, withering under Lisa's glare.

"Ooh, you know Val's mystery man, Lisa?" Lindsay said, grinning.

"Who is it?" Rachel said. "I want the wheres, whens, and hows — but especially the wheres."

"Don't tell them," Val pleaded.

"Why not? If you won't listen to *me*, then maybe your best friends can tell you why Gavin Mecozzi is bad news."

"Gavin who?"

"Oh shit," Rachel said. "I think that's Hit List Guy."

"No," Lindsay said. *"Him?"*

"Who?" Val said.

"Your boyfriend, Val — known pretty much to everyone else in the school as Hit List Guy."

"What's a hit list?"

"It's the grocery list school shooters write so they can remember who to cut down."

"Charming," Rachel said dryly.

Val blanched. "He actually made one?"

Fearscape by Nenia Campbell

It was Lindsay who answered this time. "Not exactly. It's a long story, but basically it comes down to this paper he wrote for English last year. Juniors have to read this book called *The Most Dangerous Game* by Richard Connell."

"It's a short story about this shipwrecked guy who ends up getting washed up on this island with a crazy old coot, who also happens to be an ex-hunter. And guess what? He's decided that regular game has lost its appeal — "

"Game in the hunter sense, not the playing sense," Lindsay added, for Val's benefit.

"Yeah," Rachel said. "So *he* — Count Zoloft — "

"Zaroff."

"Zoloft, Zaroff, whatever. Count *Zaroff* decides that he's going to hunt humans from now on, since they're the only worthwhile challenge left for him."

"Hit List Guy — I mean, Gavin, sorry — had some interesting things to say about that book."

"Interesting as in scared-the-shit-out-of-people."

"The teacher kept his project on display. She said it was because it was awesome and what an A-plus paper is supposed to look like, and blah, blah, blah, but everyone knew it was because the school wanted proof, in case he ever actually did something, that they weren't liable or whatever."

"Something as in shoot-up-the-school," Rachel said.

"What was the paper about?" Val asked.

"*Basically*, it was this really creepy essay about how each major clique of the school would survive, or not, if put in that kind of situation," Lisa said, seizing the conversation, "band geeks, cheerleaders, scene kids, jocks — "

"That's not a hit list, then," Val said. "I mean, it's creepy but it's not like he was actually seriously considering — "

"The cheerleaders would probably be the first to perish," Lisa said, "Because, despite their natural athleticism, they have never known what it is like to truly need to run. That's a direct quote. His essay's on the wall of my classroom. I read part of it — and had to stop."

"I've read parts of it, too," Lindsay said, nodding. "He said the most likely to survive would be one of the shy, quiet kids that nobody suspects because his or her 'apparent weakness' would cause them to be underestimated, thereby increasing his or her chance to use one of their natural advantages."

"What on earth renewed your interest in that psychopath?" Lisa wanted to know. "Because I thought we had already gone over this. Did he say something to you?"

" — exquisite," Rachel said in an undertone. Lindsay punched her in the arm.

Val wished she had something cold to put on her face. It was burning like a candle.

"Oh my God, Val," Lisa groaned. "He is going to chew you up and spit you out."

"Maybe not spit her out," Rachel said, with a leer. "Not if he likes the taste of her."

Lindsay punched her again, harder.

"Ow! Not with the lacrosse arm. That freaking hurt!"

Lisa glared at the two of them. "Val, whether you believe me or not, he will hurt you. I do not want to watch that happen."

"Hey, maybe he's a really nice guy," Rachel said, taking pity on Val's distraught expression. "I mean, Stephen King is apparently a doll and look at all the messed-up shit he writes."

But Gavin isn't nice, Val thought in despair. *He said so himself.*

She felt as if she were right smack in the face of all public scrutiny — *that's the girl who likes Hit List Guy* — and it was like being trapped in a room without doors.

■□■□■□■

When Mrs. Kimble asked, "How was school, Val?" she was a little alarmed when her normally chatty daughter responded with a grunt. "Did you have a bad day?"

"Meh," said Val.

"Meh?"

"High school is dumb." Val scrunched up her face. "Everyone is so — so *shallow*."

"Oh, Val. You say that like it's such a novel observation. High school hasn't changed much since I was a girl, and I imagine that it's been pretty much the same since public schools first began."

"It's still dumb."

"Many things in the world are, and we can't do a thing about ninety-nine-percent of them."

Val barred her arms over her chest. "I can't wait until college."

"Well, I'm afraid you're going to have to," her mother said dryly, "So I'd suggest making the best of the life you have now."

(I think you're exquisite.)

Val hesitated. "There was one good thing that happened today, though."

"Oh? What was that?"

"There's this boy at school, and I think — I really think he might like me." Val frowned again. 'Like' somehow wasn't the right word. It was too simple. Too light.

Too innocent.

Mrs. Kimble shot her a sideways grin. "Oh, that's wonderful, Baby. Is he the one you told me about earlier? The one Lisa is playing matchmaker with?"

'Playing' matchmaker? Like it's a game of pretend? Val's frowned deepened into a scowl. "No. James is a jerk."

"I see."

Silence.

"So who is this new mystery man? Did Lisa introduce you to him?"

Val stomped her foot. "Mom! I can find boys without

Lisa's help!"

"Don't stomp! And I didn't say you couldn't." Her mother looked offended.

"You implied it."

"Goodness, you're sensitive today."

Val glared ahead at the car stuck in front of them. Traffic was always heinous after school. The car had a "my child is a Derringer Honor Student" bumper sticker. The driver, however, had added another part, rife with irony, which read, "And all I got was this stupid sticker."

She bet that kid's parents didn't think they had the dating appeal of a slug.

"Oh, come on. Don't huff. Spill. I'm dying of curiosity."

Val was tempted to torture her some more — she was still quite mad about her mother's assuming that she couldn't find boys on her own, mostly because it was starting to look as if it might be true — but she was too excited to keep quiet much longer, and her mother's enthusiasm was hard to resist in the wake of Lisa's cutting skepticism.

She managed to hold out for another block until blurting, "He's a senior."

Her mother's expectant smile slipped. "Oh ... dear. So he's eighteen. That's quite old."

So are you. "That's only four years older. We go to the same high school!"

"And next year he will be in college whereas you, little missy, will still be a high school student." She rolled her eyes at her daughter's expression. "Okay, I get it. We'll discuss that later. So he's a senior. Is that all you know about him?"

"He's in my art class."

"Mm-hmm."

"He works at Petville."

Mrs. Kimble lifted an eyebrow.

"Mom!"

Mrs. Kimble demurred. "I didn't say anything."

"You looked at me."

"Oh, Val, for God's sake. I *looked* at you? How old are you?"

There was a silence.

"Well, Miss Huffy? What's this boy's name?"

Val didn't answer.

"Should we call him M&M, for Mystery Man?"

Oh god, the horror. "His name is Gavin. Gavin Mecozzi."

"That sounds Italian."

"Probably because it is."

"I knew an Italian boy growing up," her mother said thoughtfully. "He was a distant relation of a mafioso. He used to brag about that. It drove the girls crazy — that, and the fact that he looked like a young Eduardo Versategui. He also drove a Harley, as I recall, and wore a Ferragamo leather jacket."

"Gavin is *not* in the mafia."

"And what does Mr. Mecozzi do, then, in his copious free time?"

This Val could answer, to her relief. "He plays chess. He's a grandmaster."

"Well! That's certainly impressive. Your uncle plays chess. Did I ever tell you that? He used to call it 'the intellectual sport.'" The minivan pulled into their driveway. Val hopped out, slinging her backpack over one shoulder. "Your father played, too, though Charles was never as good as Earl."

"I remember. Dad tried to teach me when I was younger."

"Did he? Oh, yes, I'd quite forgotten. That all seems so long ago." As she fished in her purse for the keys, she said, casually, "What does Lisa think about this Gavin?"

"Lisa is dumb. Just like James."

As soon as her mother got the door open, Val made an immediate beeline for her room. The first thing she did was change out of her school clothes and into some flannel pajama pants and a tank top. The second was to wash off her makeup, which was starting to feel stiff and itchy. The third was to go on her computer, where she planned to stay until she was called down for dinner or ended up tired enough to take a nap on her bed.

James had finally decided to send her a message. The header was entitled, simply, "sorry." *How original.* Val deleted the message without reading it. She knew if she did read it, she would either feel sorry for him or get even more annoyed than she already was, and either one of those things had a high likelihood of making her act stupidly, herself.

Besides, he's probably only apologizing because Lisa made him.

Val had been Lisa's friend first, before Lisa really knew anyone else in the school, and she resented the fact that Lisa had gotten so tight with James lately. Especially since she was fairly sure that the two of them hung out together far more often than they bothered to include her.

Not that she wanted to hang out with such stupid people, but they could have at least offered.

She had another message, aside from James's. Val sat up a little straighter. It was from that weirdo in the Victorian outfit again.

What do you desire? And how far would you go to get it?

The time stamp was 4:21 AM.

The thought of a man lying awake in the middle of night thinking about her, and what she desired, made her feel sick — sick, and a little thrilled in an odd, frightening way.

Leave me alone, she wrote. *Why do you keep bothering me?*

The response was instantaneous.

Because you fascinate me.

What a freaky thing to say. *I fascinate you?*

Among other things.

Val hesitated. *What other things?*

A gentleman never tells.

Why are you doing this, then, you freak?

He didn't respond. Val heaved a sigh of relief as she began responding to other notifications from people she actually wanted to talk to. People who weren't freaks. She submitted a comment to one of her friends from track about the next meet, and when the screen refreshed there was another message notification waiting for her.

Because of how beautiful you are when you run — and how much it makes me want to <u>chase</u> you. The red flag flashed up again. *You never answered my question, by the way.*

His question? She scrolled back through the conversation, confused, until she hit upon the very first thing he'd sent her. What did she desire, and how far would she go to get it?

She hit the block button and turned away from her laptop.

Right now, her only desire was that her big, stupid life start making a little more sense.

Fearscape by Nenia Campbell

Chapter Five

"One of the most difficult parts of drawing from life is that you are converting a living, breathing creature into a nonliving, non-breathing format." As she talked, Ms. Wilcox went around the room and gave each pair of desks a wooden figure. "These are nonliving, non-breathing compatible, but I want you to pretend, for the moment, that they are alive, and draw them in both static — and dynamic — poses."

Val picked up the doll, adjusting the limbs so that it looked as if it were running. Several of the other students were taking far more explicit liberties with the dolls, James in particular, who shoved the doll's hand between its legs and made noises that had his seatmates in fits.

Gavin, by contrast, was quietly studying the doll he was sharing with a girl whose name Val didn't know. He had folded its limbs into a pose of supplication, the hands thrown skywards. The girl clearly didn't like it, though whether this was because she, like Val, thought it sinister, resented him taking control of the doll, or was just having trouble with the limbs wasn't clear.

Mrs. Vasquez was showing *Titus* in English so after

checking in with the teacher and getting marked as "present" on the roster, Val was sent to the library for one-day study hall. She hadn't been to the school library since the beginning of the year, and the smell of old books was overwhelming. "Hi, Ms. Banner," she said tentatively to the librarian, "I'm here for — "

Ms. Banner shushed her, with a look of annoyance, and thrust a stapled bunch of papers at her without bothering to explain them. Val glanced down at the papers with a look of wariness. *Library Rules* the first one was called, with "No Talking" underlined several times. The other three comprised her essay assignment.

Emily Abernathy was already there, seated at one of the far tables with a copy of *Wuthering Heights* in front of her. Her blonde hair was secured back with a barrette and she was wearing one of those dress and turtleneck sets that Val hadn't really seen in person since 1997. She half-wanted to peek under the table and see if she was wearing matched printed leggings.

"Hey." Emily looked up, fixing her with a shy smile that made Val feel bad about her uncharitable thought. "You're not watching the movie, either?"

"I guess not." She looked at *Wuthering Heights*. "Is that for this class? I thought we weren't reading that for another week or two."

"I'm using it in my essay," Emily said. "I'm doing my topic on revenge and betrayal within families and how the disrupting of that critical foundation of the home poisons everything. I already talked to Mrs. Vasquez, and she said it would be okay."

I'm sure she did. Val shook away that thought, appalled by her own bitchiness. "That sounds really … interesting. I'm sure you'll get an A," she tacked on hastily.

"I hope so. It's going to be hard, since I don't really like this play." Emily frowned down at her copy of *Titus Andronicus*. "What are you doing your paper on, Val?"

"I don't know. I haven't really thought about it."

And then she jumped as Ms. Banner, steadily creeping up on them this whole time, shushed.

Val grudgingly redirected her efforts into the playbook, wishing Emily hadn't said what her idea was. Now, all Val could think about was revenge — which, in turn, made her wonder if her stalker's sudden interest might be a kind of revenge on its own. But from whom? And for what? Or was she over-analyzing this?

No. There was a connection there between her own situation and the play. She pondered it on the track field, tuning out Rachel's and Lindsay's excited chatter about the French club's upcoming trip to Paris. *Titus Andronicus* was about revenge as Emily had said, but something else, too. Mrs. Vasquez had mentioned it in class, though as more of a footnote, really.

"You're so quiet today," said Lindsay. "Thinking of a certain someone?"

"Don't encourage her," Rachel said.

"I'm just trying to take an interest."

"If by 'trying to take an interest,' you mean 'nosing for information.'"

"Val, tell her that I'm only looking out for you," Lindsay protested.

"No, tell her that she's a nosier than Pinocchio with a head cold."

"Val, tell her — "

"I'm thinking about my essay," Val informed them both. "That's what I'm thinking about."

Lindsay and Rachel both exchanged a look. "Still want to take an interest?" Rachel asked.

"No, I think I'm good," Lindsay said. "I already know more than I'd like to about essays."

Blissfully, the two of them went back to their conversation, which made Val remember the lecture topic which had fled her mind.

The castration of women.

Mrs. Vasquez had said that Lavinia's rape and mutilation symbolized complete and utter impotence as Lavinia was prevented from speaking for herself in the most frighteningly literal sense. She had ceased to be a person, and had instead become an object. Voiceless. Helpless.

The first time they had read that passage in class, Val became so nauseated that she begged for the bathroom pass. Instead of going to the bathrooms, however, she stood in the breezeway between her building and the next, trying to will such gruesome imagery from her head as the wind chilled the sweat on her skin. It would have been better if it were fantasy, if people were incapable of being so sick and cruel and violent, but it wasn't fantasy and it did happen — and that made vicious psychopaths far more chilling than any monster.

Val remembered this, in particular, when she opened her locker and a cascade of rose petals poured out, the fetid stink of their sweetness nearly suffocating in its potency. Red petals, salted with the star-shaped blossoms of white jasmine. "Oh god," she breathed, staring at the flowers in horror. Her locker had been just that — locked.

Quickly, she began grabbing them by the fistful and throwing them in the trashcan, noticing as she did that the petals were fresh and hadn't even begun to wilt. An observation that made goosebumps erupt up and down her arms. She stared into the darkness, terrified that she would see nothing and even more terrified that she wouldn't.

And then she heard a metallic sound, which made her start, jerkily, back towards her locker. It was just the squeak of the door's hinges as it swung open a little further from her frenzied gestures. But that wasn't what commanded her attention. Her eyes were riveted on the inside of the door — or, more specifically, what was carved there.

Gouged into the metal, by a cruel blade and a crueler hand, was one word. One word, and yet its connotations numbered in the thousands.

MINE.

It was with a trembling hand she traced the 'E.' The metal edges were ragged and sliced open her finger, leaving a bead of blood on the letter's bottom bar. The pain shattered the dissociation and the dreaminess Val felt, and all at once she was no longer removed from the situation. This wasn't fantasy; this was real — and it had just turned deadly.

Val closed her fingers into a fist, hiding the blood, and screamed as loud as she could, "Mrs. Freeman!"

■□■□■□■

Coach Freeman was sympathetic but there was not much she could do. For obvious reasons, no security cameras were permitted in the locker rooms, though there were some facing the two outer doors. She employed the first-aid kit for the cut on Val's hand and offered her a new locker and combination, but apart from that Val found herself pretty much on her own.

Which was unpleasant but not unexpected. If he was devious enough to get into her locker, she saw no reason why he shouldn't be devious enough to escape being caught.

Had he been watching her reaction? Savoring it? The answered seemed to be yes, because when Val got home, frazzled and a little sweaty from the walk from the bus stop, there was another message waiting for her.

That wasn't very polite.

It had been sent mere minutes before.

What wasn't? She typed, knowing it was foolish but unable to help herself.

Disposing of my gift so callously.

Gift? *That wasn't a gift. That was vandalism.*

I can assure you, my dear, that I am no garden-variety reprobate.

A chill slithered down her spine. No high school student talked like that. *Do you go to my high school?* She paused. *Are you a teacher?*

Everyone has something that they would like to teach.

Was that a yes? A no? Either way, it wasn't reassuring.

Why do you keep bothering me?

Because I have something that I would like to teach you.

What, how to act like a creepy pervert? *Leave me alone*, she wrote. *I don't want to learn ANYTHING from you.* Val swallowed, her eyes glued to the screen as she waited for the response.

She didn't wait long.

You don't have a choice.

Val yelped, and blocked him. This couldn't really be happening. Things like this didn't happen outside of horror movies and creepy plays. *Right?*

Another message popped up from a different user, but with the same picture.

You can't escape from me, Valerian. I want you — and very soon I intend to catch you. To cage you. To make you mine. Forever.

STOP TALKING TO ME.

Mockingly, the messages continued to arrive, *And who knows, Val —*

"Mom!"

You may even find, given time, that you don't want to resist my control.

"What is it, Val?"

After all, dominance can be a very potent aphrodisiac.

"This guy — " Val could barely speak. "This guy keeps

sending me messages."

Mrs. Kimble frowned, concerned but also puzzled. "Did you block him?"

"I did, but he won't stop. I'm scared — the things he sends me, they're, well, scary. Look — " Val pointed at the screen, backing up in her chair so her mother could read the message. She wondered if she might throw up.

"Oh — oh my God," Mrs. Kimble said. "I'll call your father — "

"No!" Val cried. "Don't! I don't want Dad to see this. Don't let him!"

"All right, Val, but ..." she put her hands on her daughter's shoulders, "when did this start? Is this the first time this has happened?"

"Someone defaced my locker at school," she sniffed. *And watches me when I run.* But she didn't say that, because she know her mother would call Coach Freeman, then, and have her suspended from the team. And apart from Art, and her own limited social circle, track pretty much made up her entire social life. "Is it — is it my fault, do you think?"

"No, I don't. He sounds disturbed. But don't respond to

him anymore. That was foolish of you to do. He probably took it as encouragement," she added darkly, "Men like that do."

"Then what *do* I do?"

"Ignore him, and he'll lose interest."

"But what if he sends me another message?"

"Block him. Don't even dignify it with a response or an excuse. Just keep blocking him. And if he creates a new account to bother you with, block that one, too."

Val stared dismally at the screen. "Okay …." *But I don't think that's going to help.*

"And change your profile picture," Mrs. Kimble added. "I've told you a thousand times, Valerian, that it isn't appropriate for someone your age. Look at you — half-naked."

"But it's just my track uniform," Val protested. "It covers more than a swimsuit."

"Don't argue with me. Just change your picture and for God's sake, don't respond to him."

■□■□■□■

True to her word, Mrs. Kimble didn't show Val's father the Facebook messages — *probably because she knows she doesn't have access to my account,* Val thought — but she heard the two of them discussing it after dinner in worried undertones. Without her. They were talking about Val as if she didn't even live under the same roof.

No. Worse. As if the situation doesn't even concern me. It's my life. It's happening to me!

She ended up locking herself in her room and calling Lisa, mad or no. Val needed to talk about this with somebody her own age or she felt like she would go insane. She would have preferred Rachel or Lindsay, but for the same reasons she was also afraid to talk to them. They were older and more mature. They might think she was stupid and naïve for getting herself into this mess in the first place, and Val didn't want them to think badly of her, too.

Lisa answered on the first ring. "Go *away*, Mom! It's for me! Hello? Val?"

"Hey. I wanted to talk. Is that okay?"

"Just as long as you don't expect me to giggle over Gavin with you like a giddy schoolgirl."

"Lisa, don't be a bitch, this is serious and if you can't be serious I'm going to hang up!"

"I'm just saying. But anyway," she went on, "what did you want to tell me?"

"Some creep is following me and I don't know who — or why. He's always sending me messages about how much he wants to, I don't know, *own* me, and today he broke into my locker and filled it with flowers and carved the word 'mine' into the door with a knife." Val's voice broke. "I think he's watching me on the track field, too, but I can't tell my mom or she might call the coach and have them take me off. I'm scared, Lisa, and I don't know what to do."

"God," Lisa said reverently, "and you have no idea who it is?"

"No," said Val.

Lisa clicked her tongue. "It's like something out of a movie. Remember that one — "

"This isn't a movie, Lisa, and I'm freaking out because he seems to know a whole lot about my schedule, and a whole bunch of other stuff about me. I'm really starting to think that he might do something. *Try* something. You know?"

"I'm sorry." Thoughtful silence. "I know! I'll tell James to eat with us at lunch. He's big."

"It's not lunchtime that freaks me out," said Val, "It's when I'm *alone*."

"Oh. Well. Have you ever stopped to consider that it might be Lover Boy? He's unhinged."

"*Lisa —* "

"Okay. Fine. It's not him. Who is it then? What does he want? And why from you?"

Val hugged her knees to her chest, leaning back against her fuzzy pillow. "I wish I knew."

"I'd still bring it up with Gavin. See what he says, and whether or not he acts guilty. He's who I'd suspect."

"You're just saying that because you don't like him."

"No, I don't, and you shouldn't, either."

"Lisa!" Val closed her eyes. "Look. I also called you because I wanted to ask you for help."

"Help with what?"

"You know everyone. Well … almost everyone. Everyone in our grade, anyway. Will you see what you can find out, or if anyone's mad at me? I wouldn't even know where to begin."

"Oh, sure. Of course!"

Val had a horrific image of Lisa peering through a

magnifying glass like a grotesquely teenybopper version of Nancy Drew — in jeggings. "Don't tell anyone," she added quickly. "I don't want anyone to know. I mean it. If you tell anyone, I'll stop being your friend."

"But what if someone wants to know why I'm asking weird questions?"

"Don't be that obvious."

"Easy for you to say." Val could hear the eye roll in her friend's voice. "I'll do my best."

"Thanks …."

"You know, your stalker reminds me of Erik, from *The Phantom of the Opera*."

"The movie?" Val asked, immediately thinking of Gerard Butler.

"No. The book. He was a lot more twisted in the book. Less romantic and tragic and sad. He even had a torture chamber."

"You're really not making me feel better, you know!"

"Sorry. I just think it's a weird coincidence. I mean, the Phantom wanted Christine because he thought she had a beautiful voice, right? This guy wants you because he thinks you look beautiful when you run." Lisa paused. "Weird, really, how a guy could take an innocent hobby and incorporate it into some twisted fantasy about sex and saving grace — you know?"

"It's creepy," Val said, in a tiny voice. "I don't like it. Being watched all the time. Or feeling like I am. It's just as bad, either way. I miss feeling safe when I'm alone."

"Hey — *The Phantom of the Opera* ended happily enough."

"This isn't a *movie*, Lisa! And even if my stalker *did* look like Gerard Butler, I'd still freak out."

"I don't think you have to worry about that," Lisa said. "Him looking like Gerard Butler, I mean. Most likely he's a gross nerd with a small dick."

Val hung up on her without preamble. She let Lisa call her back three times before deigning to pick up the phone and let her apologize.

Chapter Six

Ms. Wilcox wasn't even there when Val arrived at her classroom, and yet the door was wide open. Probably because of the janitor. Technically, students weren't supposed to be alone in a classroom without the teacher present but Val was pretty sure nobody had seen her, and even if they had, she could always say that the teacher had only stepped out for a second or that she thought the janitor counted as faculty — which they did, surely?

She sat down at an empty table, inhaling the smell of paint. More important, she needed the time and silence to contemplate how she was going to talk to Gavin. She had a feeling that, *Hi, are you the guy stalking me on Facebook?* wasn't going to cut it.

Maybe she should just ask him if he had a Facebook and work from there.

Do you cosplay? Do you participate in historical reenactments? Do you like putting on creepy costumes while scaring the hell out of your classmates?

She really was terrible at this, wasn't she? She sucked at being manipulative. If Gavin was guilty, he'd know immediately what she was getting at, which would be bad. If he wasn't guilty, he'd just think she was a freak, and that would be bad, too.

Grateful that nobody was around to see her embarrassment, Val set her backpack down on the desk and basked in the silence. Without the new-age music Ms. Wilcox was so fond of playing, Val could focus on the details she generally ignored in the face of the sensory overload which resulted from a large class-size. The sour tang of paint, the earthy wood of the carving blocks, the way the trees outside caused the light on the floors to dapple. Dust motes in the air caught and reflected the early morning light, sparking like burning embers and reminding Val of faerie dust.

Magic.

Art was magic, in a way. Each drawing was a window into the mind that created it.

Val pulled her sketchbook from its canvas prison and fished around the bottom of her backpack until she located her fine-tipped pens and charcoal pencils. Expensive, the lot of them, but the difference in quality from ordinary pens and pencils was extraordinary.

The first drawing in Val's sketchbook was her earliest attempt at sketching: a very sad-looking animal which resembled a horse but was actually supposed to be her neighbor's black Lab, Chocolate. If it were up to her she would have balled it up and thrown the drawing away, but Ms. Wilcox said that throwing away mistakes was forbidden.

"Otherwise, how can you be sure you won't do it again?" She said, when she caught Val trying to tear out the page. "Keep it. Learn from it."

So the ugly picture, partially torn from her book, continued to remain in Val's portfolio to taint the rest of her collection and embarrass her every time she looked at it. She stuck out her tongue at the dog-horse, whose tongue was also sticking out, and flipped through the pages — flowers, hands, feet, tree — until she came to the sketch that she wanted to work on.

This drawing, also unfinished, was of an old warehouse that lay on the edge of the town perimeter. Mrs. Kimble thought the building was an eyesore that ought to be replaced by a new, sparkling facade similar to that of Derringer's newly renovated downtown, which had been refurbished to look like what *The Derringer Tattle* referred to as a "west coast Cambridge."

But Val liked this building, rundown as it was. The crumbling roof tiles and boarded-up windows gave it character; it was a building one might take a picture of on Instagram and then tag with an inspirational quote. She also liked her drawing, in spite of its flaws. It might not have the same charm as a saturated photograph, but it was hers, and contained part of her in it.

She selected one of the sharper pencils and began shading in the grass in the shadow of the rusted chain-link fence. She was aware of someone sitting down in the desk besides hers, but only distantly, and she didn't look up. She was too intent on trying to recapture that juxtaposition of shadow and light, of color and contrast, in her mind's eye.

"Chiaroscuro."

The word rolled off the speaker's tongue with easy fluency.

Val jumped, and all the red that had vanished only minutes before flooded back into her face with a vengeance as she realized who was sitting beside her. He was leaning on his hand, watching her draw, though his eyes went back to her face when she stopped.

"What you're doing there. That's what it's called." He nodded at her drawing. "Chiaroscuro. The contrast of light and dark. I didn't mean to startle you. You've ruined your drawing."

Val cursed when she saw the scribble she'd inadvertently scratched into the pad. "It'll erase," she muttered, rubbing at it, hoping that it would. "I'm surprised you remember."

"There was an assignment on it just two weeks ago."

Oh. He was right. Val stopped rubbing. Crap.

"Then again, I am TA. It's my job to remember."

"TA?" She stared at his sketchbook, then at his face. "That's right. I remember now you told me in the …."

Wait. He was TA — so did that mean he'd graded her work? She thought of all the assignments she'd turned in and tried to remember if any of them were stupid or lame. God, he probably thought she was a total idiot, regardless; she couldn't come up with anything to say.

"You're still allowed to participate?" she said at last.

"I draw for fun. I've taken this class twice before — I can't take it for normal credit anymore."

"Oh." She stared down at her white freckled hands, smeared black from the charcoals. *Chiaroscuro.* She wouldn't be forgetting now.

A sudden bustling at the door made both teens look up. Ms. Wilcox, who had always reminded Val vaguely of Ms. Frizzle from the Magic School Bus, was incapable of entering a room quietly. Her blonde hair was frizzy and wild, held in place with a plastic purple clip in the shape of a daisy.

She set her battered satchel down in its usual spot behind her desk and inserted one of her all-instrumental CDs into the player. Panpipes and lutes filled the classroom and Val lost the nerve to keep talking. "Good morning," their teacher sang out. "You two are early today."

Val realized, with a jolt, that before Ms. Wilcox had entered she and Gavin had been the only two people in the classroom.

"Gavin, I know. And you are … Valerie?"

"Valerian. Val."

"Val," Ms. Wilcox agreed. "I knew that part, at least. That picture you did of the little kittens was absolutely wonderful,

Val. You've improved so much since the beginning of the semester."

"Thank you."

"I hope you'll consider taking my advanced class."

Val was painfully aware of Gavin's appraising stare. "We'll see. I've got a lot of, um, required classes to take."

"There's certainly no rush. You have years ahead of you, yet. And on that note, Mr. Mecozzi, I've just about finished with your letter of recommendation. Three sealed copies, and one for your own personal viewing pleasure."

"You're too kind."

"Such politeness. It's like a comedy of manners." Ms. Wilcox glanced at the door. "I hope the other students show your foresight in coming early. Today's assignment is going to be rather time-consuming. It may well cut into tomorrow's lesson. If you like, you can start on it now."

"What is it?" Val asked.

"Since we worked from wooden figures last class I thought it might be nice to draw actual living, breathing figures today." Val nodded and turned to a blank page in her sketchbook. That sounded innocent enough.

"Oh, but you'll need a partner. You'll be drawing someone from this class, so I suppose you will have to wait, after all." Her eyes lit on the boy beside Val. "Unless … Gavin, would you mind terribly being Val's partner for today?"

"It would be my pleasure," he said solemnly, rising.

"I don't want to bother — "

"It's no trouble," Ms. Wilcox assured her. "Is it, Gavin?"

"Not at all."

"There, you see? Why don't you two go outside. The light's better. It's a lovely day out."

Val was relieved. She wouldn't have to deal with James. She had been afraid of him asking her about his still-unread Facebook message and making her look like a total hypocrite to boot. Now she could avoid him for another day.

She had to trot alongside Gavin to keep up with his long strides. It made her feel as if she were one of those annoying little dogs, nipping at his heels. "How tall are you?" she asked.

"Six-four," he replied.

Around them, students milled about, biding their time until final bell. Val tried to find a quiet place for them to draw; it gave her a good excuse not to look at him.

"Do you have a Facebook?"

"Were you looking for me?"

She ducked her head. "No. I mean — I was just wondering."

Gavin shook his head. "I don't have the time to bother."

Now that sounded like a brush-off. *Maybe he isn't interested in me, after all.* He seemed distracted, his eyes distant. *At least that would mean he's not my stalker.*

But she couldn't help feeling a little disappointed.

"Where would you like to sketch me?"

"How about the grass between the six-hundred and seven-hundred buildings? There's some interesting light there. I can do you against the tree."

She regretted the words the instant they were out of her mouth. Gavin's eyes widened, and then he throw back his head and laughed. Not one of those quietly sardonic chuckles that had annoyed her so much in the cafe, but an out-and-out guffaw.

"Stop it," Val snapped, trying not to fixate on how sexy his laugh was. "That isn't what I meant."

His laughter subsided somewhat and he said in an

amused tone, "I gathered."

"Good."

"I'm surprised you're speaking to me."

Val was beginning to question the same thing. "How do you mean?"

"Didn't your friend warn you away from me?"

Well, that was unexpected. She was thrown. "Why do you care? You weren't very nice to her."

"I like knowing what people say about me behind my back."

That made him the only one then. She shrugged her shoulders. "She tried."

"It didn't work?"

"I like finding things out for myself."

His head swung in her direction; for better or for worse, she'd managed to get his attention. A slow smile crawled over his lips like a spider, and it was both frightening and seductive. "Curiosity can be a very dangerous thing, my dear."

My dear? "Why? Are you saying she was right? Are you going to take a turn at in now?"

"At warning you away?" His lips twitched back into a normal semblance of a smile and she wondered if what she had seen — or thought she had seen — had been nothing more than an illusion caused by the throw of shadows on his face from the curtain of leaves above. "I believe I'd rather let you, oh, what was it — do me against the tree."

Val didn't trust herself to speak. Unwilling to set her sketchpad down on the slightly damp grass she juggled her drawing supplies, trying to find the most comfortable position to draw. She ended up sitting with her legs folded crosswise, so she could balance the sketchpad on her knees.

Gavin leaned back against the tree trunk, facing her, with his long legs stretched out. He bent one, off which to hang his arm, and said, teasingly, "How do you want me?"

Those words made the heat rush to her face again — God, he was a jerk, wasn't he, trying to fluster her on purpose like this — and she said, gratingly, "Relaxed. Natural."

"Those aren't necessarily mutually inclusive."

"Whatever is natural for *you* then."

Val braced herself for more dalliance and teasing. To her relief he said only, "I can do that. May I?" Without waiting for a response he removed his glasses, setting them carefully down on the ground beside him before reassuming his position. His eyes closed, his breathing slowed, and his posture — it changed. She couldn't say how — it was a subtle change — but noticeable nonetheless because he no longer looked the same ….

A breeze blew through the grass, ruffling his hair and making ripples in his white shirt. Beneath his unbuttoned collar she could make out some kind of necklace composed of heavy silver links. He regarded her through half-closed eyes, and while he seemed perfectly content in this lackadaisical slouch his entire body seemed a heartbeat away from springing into motion.

He was striking.

Much too unusual-looking to be considered handsome in the classical sense, but eye-catching all the same. He had the kind of face that would cause her mother to nod at and say, knowledgeably, "He'll grow into his looks."

Val swallowed and lowered her eyes to her sketchbook, no longer able to keep contact with his. Not while he was looking at her like that.

Soon she had a pretty good outline of his body. Broad shoulders, finely corded throat. She looked at him in pieces, too afraid to see the whole. High cheekbones. Roman nose. His eyes had gradually wandered up the tree to watch the small sparrows cavorting in the branches above but apart from that he was eerily still. *But alert*, she thought, *almost like a predator at rest.*

Silly thought. But then his eyes snapped back and she felt her heart flutter uneasily as some innate fear responded to her unsettling perception of him.

Didn't your friend warn you away?

Why had he said such things to her? Didn't he know about the rumors? Yes, of course he did. He'd admitted as much himself. So then why would he bring it up? To clear the waters?

Or to drag her under?

"You have an intriguing expression on your face, Val."

"It's nothing. Don't talk."

"Is something wrong?"

"Everything's fine. I was just thinking about something I have to do."

"Against the tree?"

"No." Val blushed angrily. That was just a little too close to the truth. "Stop talking."

"You blush very easily," he remarked, stretching and subsequently causing the fabric of his shirt to pull taut against his chest in a movement that seemed far too graceful and calculated to be accidental. "It's rather hard to resist, you know."

It's not the only thing. It felt like all the saliva in her mouth had evaporated. *I do like him. Oh God. This is bad.*

"I think we had better get back to class," he said, still watching her with amusement.

"But the bell hasn't rung yet," said Val.

"It will any second now."

A splitting blare cut through the quadrangle, muffling his last word. She looked at him. "How did you do that?"

"Magic."

"Really."

"A magician never tells. May I see the drawing?"

She cursed whichever Irish ancestor gave her this mood ring of a skin condition. "When it's done. A magician never tells." She raised the pitch of her voice, mocking him.

He smiled. "Fair enough."

She watched him pick up his glasses and adjust them on his face. "So what do you draw? Since you can't take this class for credit. Do you get to draw whatever you want?"

"Within reason," he said, "though I try to follow the lesson plan along with everyone else."

Val had trouble believing that. He did not strike her as a rule-follower. Or any kind of follower, for that matter. "What do you draw?" she asked, "for your own entertainment?"

"Animals, mostly."

"What else?"

He gave her a sideways grin. "The chessboard Ms. Wilcox used in her chiaroscuro lecture."

Haltingly, she said, "That was yours? I thought — " *I thought it was professional, real.*

"I played." He admitted this as casually as other boys owned up to sports. "It was easy."

Val caught herself bobbing her head in agreement and checked herself. She wasn't supposed to know that he was a master. "Chess, or drawing it?"

His smile widened. "Both."

"Do you draw people?"

"Not usually."

"So sometimes, then."

"When I find a subject that arouses my interest, then yes. But I prefer animals. They don't have the same unfortunate tendency to pose, and are much easier to work with. The next class will be an exception to my rule, however."

"What's the occasion?"

"I'll be drawing you."

"Me?" It came out as a yelp.

"We trade places, remember?" He placed her pens, which she had forgotten in the long blades of grass, into her hand, closing her fingers lightly around them. "It'll be my turn to do you against the tree, or other applicable surface."

Val, at this moment, understood suddenly what the life of a radiator must be like.

"Careful," Gavin said. "If you keep blushing like that, I may do more than just draw you."

And with that one remark he turned, leaving her standing there in the quad as it slowly began to fill up with students as she watched his departing back. It sounded like a suggestion. It also sounded, vaguely, like a threat. That was when Val knew that she was in trouble: because she didn't really care, either way.

Chapter Seven

During the bus ride to school, Val felt extremely apprehensive. The weekend had given her plenty of time to amass her doubts, primarily sown by Lisa, and now they had taken root and sprouted, seeping so deeply into her brain that, like weeds, she could never be entirely sure whether she'd successfully chased them out.

Was Gavin her stalker?

Did her stalker want to hurt her?

Did *Gavin* want to hurt her?

They marched on — an endless array of questions, each as poisonous and vicious as a hydra. And, like the hydra, it seemed that as soon as Val managed to slay one question several more spawned to fill its place.

Would she have been so quick to suspect Gavin if he had been popular?

No. Popular people tended to think like everyone else. It made them less interesting to be around, less exciting, but it also made them less likely to stalk people — or hurt people.

Hurt *her*.

Val rubbed at her tummy and leaned back against the

seat. She'd forgone breakfast that morning in favor of stealing one of her father's carbonated lemon-flavored waters in the hopes that something innocuous and familiar would help settle her stomach.

It hadn't.

She found the art classroom empty except for Gavin, who was behind the teacher's desk, typing something at the computer. "What are you doing?" she asked.

"Just entering some grades and things," he said vaguely. "Are you ready to pose for me?"

Val took a sip of her water. The bubbles stung her chapped lips. "Shouldn't we wait? For Mrs. Wilcox, I mean?"

"I spoke to her earlier this morning."

"Oh. Okay." Val picked up her things, aware of his eyes on her.

"You can't get away so easily." He stood up from the desk and stretched. "You seem different, by the way. Subdued, almost. Are you all right?"

"I don't feel well."

"Hmm." He held open the door for her. "I'll try not to overexert you, then."

Fearscape by Nenia Campbell

They walked across the quad. She found herself looking around, wondering if people had noticed her and Gavin together. Nobody she could see was watching, and she knew that on a rational level it was likely nobody would, but being around him made Val hyper-aware of everything. Him, especially. Even if she'd chosen not to abide by them, Lisa's warnings still rang quite clearly in her mind.

(I'd still bring it up with Gavin. See what he says, and if he acts guilty. He's who I'd suspect.)

He certainly didn't act guilty. He didn't betray any emotions at all. Even the various rumors of which he was the subject didn't seem to faze him. Val had never met anyone before who was so detached from other people's thoughts and actions. Was someone like that even capable of looking guilty or feeling guilt at all?

(He scares people.)

Despite her claims to the contrary, Val was very much influenced by the opinions of others and for all Gavin's politeness and charm, there was something dark gathered around him as if he were the epicenter of a brewing storm.

He frightened her, and yet she couldn't stay away.

"Against the tree?" His voice sliced through her thoughts like a hot knife through butter.

"Um, sure." He had led her to the same place as before. She had followed him so blindly she hadn't even noticed. *I didn't even see where we were going.* "Standing or sitting?"

"Sitting, I think, since you said you didn't feel well." He studied her, then tapped his sketchpad with his pencil. "Take off your coat."

"It's chilly out."

As she spoke the words a breeze rustled the leaves and her hair, as if in agreement. Winter had long since yielded to spring, but very reluctantly.

"I can't draw you bundled up like that." He sat about six feet away with his own coat flared out behind him like a pair of black wings adding, "It isn't as if I asked you to strip for me."

"I never said anything about that, just that it was cold!"

"Your thoughts are written all over your face." He paused. "Why, Val, what an interesting shade of scarlet you're turning."

She yanked her arms out of the side and tossed it aside.

"There," she growled. "Satisfied?"

"Always, with you," was his soft response, which made her feel embarrassed for letting her emotions get the better of her like a child. He smiled fleetingly and commenced drawing.

Val closed her eyes and tried not to move. She was so nervous that her hands were shaking. She shifted them to her lap where it would be less noticeable. There was a chill in the air despite the sun, and it grew colder and steadily more biting in the shade of the mulberry tree.

"Don't move," he said, when she shivered.

It was funny, how easy being still was at home when you were daydreaming at the window or reading a good book, but how hard it was while in the presence of someone who made you feel … odd. It didn't help, either, that he was far more at ease than her.

He had positioned her against the same tree but with her legs bent at a demure angle, her head tilted slightly back. She'd made the decision to close her eyes since she had no hope of attempting the stare-down he'd given her last time, and he didn't seem to consider it an impediment to his drawing — thank God.

"Tilt your head back more," he said, "and then slightly to the side. Stop fidgeting."

She clenched her hands tighter in her lap.

"Beautiful," she thought he said, and this was so faint she wondered if she had imagined it.

After what felt like eternity, but couldn't have been more than ninety minutes, he said, "You can relax now. I'm just about done."

Her whole body seemed to sigh in relief. She got up too fast and stumbled a little, only to feel his steadying hand on her back, just at the base of her spine. His eyes were dark, thrown into shadow cast by his facing away from the sun. "Are you all right?"

He smelled like roses and sandalwood and boy. "Um — "

The arm around her waist tightened. "Would you like to see?"

"Excuse me?" There was something wrong with her ears.

"Here."

Oh — the drawing.

She peered at the sketchbook, not entirely sure what she

expected to see. Only that it filled with a doubt that bordered on dread, and was so intense it left her breathless. But it was just a simple picture of her, sitting under the tree, formed by soft lines in charcoal pencil. He'd captured something of her in that sketch of his, though. Something that blurred the lines between what she was, versus what he wanted her to be, between sensible and sensual, between fact and fiction.

She raised her eyes. They were worried. "Is this how you see me?"

"At that moment, yes," he said.

And something about that phrasing gave her pause, though she said, "It's good."

"It will be better when it's colored but I imagine that the color of your hair will be difficult to capture on paper."

The hair on the back of her neck prickled in alarm.

"Val? You've gone pale."

It was the sun that was bothering her. Eclipsed by his face, the sun had gone black.

She must have closed her eyes, because when she opened them again she found herself lying on the ground. Gavin's face was above hers, curious, but dispassionate. Surely that couldn't be right, though, because then he noticed her looking and smiled, stroking her cheek.

"You fainted for a moment there."

She brought her hands to her throbbing temples. "I feel so dizzy."

"Mm-hmm."

"Is that why my ears were ringing? It feels like they're packed with cotton." She stuck a finger in her ear and wiggled it a little, but he lowered her hand back to her side.

"It sounds like you had a panic attack."

"A panic attack?" she repeated. "But I wasn't panicking —"

"Mere anxiety can be enough. What were you thinking about?"

"About my stalker."

"Oh?"

Her throat contracted as she looked up. His expression hadn't changed.

"I have a stalker. He's really sick. He sends me these messages —"

"About?"

Was there more than just innocent curiosity behind that single word? "Sexual things." She looked away. Just thinking about it made her feel sick. "I don't want to talk about it."

"What did you eat this morning?"

She blinked. "Um. Nothing. Just water — with lemon."

"Ah. Lemon juice lowers your blood pressure," he explained. "That, combined with stress. I'm not at all surprised you fainted. In fact, it's rather impressive you holding up as long as you did."

Val didn't feel impressive. She felt like an idiot.

"I imagine you don't want to return to class."

She made a noise of agreement.

"And since we're already late for second period — " he spread his coat on the ground " — why not rest here? I see you've already got your things. That makes it a bit simpler."

"Aren't you going to ask me if I want to go to the nurse?"

"Do you?"

"No, but — "

"Then it doesn't matter." He leaned back. "Does it?"

Val stared at him. He was so strange. "Don't you have a class to go to?"

"Biology. They won't miss me."

"Oh." The wind lifted a strand of her hair. She batted it aside impatiently. "English for me."

"What are you reading?"

"*Wuthering Heights*. We just finished *Titus*." Val let her tone convey her impressions of it.

"You didn't like it?"

"Did *you*?"

"Oh, yes. It's one of my favorite Shakespearean plays. '*We hunt not, we, with horse nor hound, / But hope to pluck a dainty doe to ground.*' The writing is quite beautiful."

"Ugh, no, it's awful." Val rolled onto her side. "Why do you talk like that?"

"Hmm?"

"You sound like one of the characters in the books we read in English."

"Is that a compliment, or an insult?"

"It's weird." She shook her head. "Normal people don't talk like that."

"I think we've already established that I'm not like other people."

"I don't know you well enough to say."

"And would you like to? Know me better?"

Her eyes skittered over him, and then away. "I don't know." Their conversation was making her feel cold and fluttery. When he was quoting that play she felt as if she were in free-fall, caught between weightlessness and a lethal plunge.

He moved closer and she lay, frozen, as the rough pads of his fingers traced her lower lip. "Why don't you meet my eyes?"

Reluctantly she did so. "I don't know."

"I doubt that." His fingers slid down her jawline. "I know what people say about me. I hear the same rumors as you." She stiffened when his hand closed lightly around the back of her neck. "Some of them are even true." His voice, which had been lowering all this time, finished at a whisper.

Val had started to break eye contact again but at his words she focused on him with alarm. "Which ones?"

"I'm dangerous."

"You are?"

"Very."

She wet her lips. "Like, to me?"

"Especially you." He regarded her through eyes shuttered against the sunlight.

"Maybe I could use some danger," she said uncertainly.

"And if I told you that I wanted to hurt you?" His voice was curious, interested.

The sunlight on her skin became a spiderweb of golden ice. "Hurt me?"

He leaned up, then, briefly catching her lower lip between his teeth before moving closer to seal his lips against hers. Soon her head was tilted so far back that her neck was slightly arched. "You've never even been kissed before, have you?"

Val let out a small gasp when he moved down her throat and she felt the sting of his teeth in her earlobe. It made her shudder and she felt the puffs of his breathy laughter. "You're so innocent." And the sibilant words tickled unpleasantly when he whispered into her ear, "You should run from me while you can."

She was breathing too hard and to her chagrin it wasn't entirely from fear. "Or what?"

The smile he gave her as he pulled away was like an

arrow in her heart. "I catch you."

■□■□■□■

Every time she looked into those graphite eyes she experienced a frisson of emotion. But it was a pale shadow of the overwhelming reaction she experienced when looking into his eyes for real. Her stomach still quivered when she remembered their interaction from earlier that day.

She could still feel his lips, soft and warm and rough, on hers.

"Why are you staring at your sketchbook like that?"

"N-no reason!" Val slammed it closed, darting a quick smile at Lisa. "Just a sketch."

Lisa wrinkled her nose. "You're acting sketchy."

"I am not acting sketchy!"

"If you were acting any sketchier, you'd be in a sketch*book*," Lisa said. "Just so you know, James is going to eat with us today, and he'll take it personally if you're acting funny after your behavior from before."

"Why is James sitting with us?"

"Because of your stalker, remember? Weren't you just telling me how you wanted a big, strong man around to protect you at lunchtime?"

"No," Val grated. "Those were your words. You said that. Why didn't you tell me he was coming?"

"Only because I knew you'd pitch a fit. Don't even think about running away. Be a big girl."

Val shoved her sketchpad into her backpack and took a resentful bite of sandwich. "You suck."

"James is as much my friend as you are. It's not easy, looking after both your interests." Val muttered something rebellious and sarcastic which Lisa choose to ignore. "By the way, where's the gruesome twosome?"

"*Rachel* and *Lindsay* are at French Club."

"Ooh la la." Lisa tilted her head, causing her hair to flow in a perfect waterfall over one shoulder. "Gay Paree."

Val slammed down her sandwich. "Lisa! For God's sake — "

"Oh look," she said, neatly cutting Val off, "there's James. Hi, James!"

James waved back, looking around a little nervously at the stares Lisa's manic waving was generating. "Hey." He sat across from Lisa at a diagonal from Val. He gave the two of them an easy smile before launching into his turkey and gravy.

Val eyed the mess with distaste. She didn't trust meals drenched in sauce.

Or the people who ate them.

"What's up?"

Val sipped her juice primly, leaving Lisa to settle the score on that one. The latter looked at Val, only mildly annoyed, before saying, "I got a C on that crummy English paper. Apparently the book ending is different from the movie ending. Oops."

James made a face. "I hate it when that happens. But you're in honors, right?"

"That doesn't mean I don't get lazy," Lisa said, rolling her eyes.

"What was the book?"

"Phantom of the Opera. I was *almost* finished but then Gossip Girl came on and of course I had to watch it, but it was on late and I fell asleep. So I just watched the ending of the movie on Youtube on my iPhone while my mom drove me to school this morning."

Val continued to drink her juice. That was safer than

commenting.

"What do girls see in that show?"

"It's a good show!"

"My ex made me watch it and I never saw the point. Bunch of rich girls sitting around and talking about where their shoes came from. Weak."

"There's not supposed to be a point," said an irate Lisa. "It's just fun."

"Fun for you, maybe. What about you, Val?" James asked. "Are you into that trash, too?"

"Oh, Val is beyond that," Lisa said, before Val could reply. "She and Hit List Guy are apparently a thing no — *ow*! Val, what the hell? That fucking hurt!"

Val had launched a kick to her alleged friend's leg beneath the table. "You promised!"

"I didn't think you meant James," Lisa protested, rubbing her shin.

"When I said don't tell anybody, I meant don't tell anybody!"

"Hit List Guy?" James broke in. "That weird senior? The one who everyone thought was going to blow up the school?

You're going out with *him*?"

"He has a name."

"Yeah, well, he also gave me a D-minus on my midterm art project. So I don't really care."

"He's your TA?" Lisa said, darting a look at Val.

"Unfortunately."

"What did you draw?"

"My ball and glove. He said it lacked *insight*. I was like, the fuck? It's a ball and glove. They don't feel anything. Thank God we've moved onto people now."

He turned back to Val.

"Hey, where were you today? And yesterday, too? I didn't see you."

"I was outside. Ms. Wilcox let me start on my assignment early."

"Oh." James frowned. "But we needed partners for that assignment, didn't we?"

"I had a partner."

"But everyone else was — " he broke off, comprehension dawning in his face. "Oh."

"Oh?" Lisa's eyes widened. "Wait — Hit List is your

partner?"

"Gavin," Val interjected coldly.

"I see. So that's why you were staring at your sketchbook. You've got a picture of him in there, don't you? You do!" she said triumphantly, glimpsing Val's reddening face. "Ooh, I want to see."

"Stop it, Lisa."

"Does he pose for you?" Lisa paused, "Is he *naked*?"

Val leaped off the bench, yanking her backpack away as Lisa made a playful grab for it. "I said cut it out! Leave me alone!"

Lisa dropped her arm. "Val…"

"Why are you giving me such a hard time?" Val demanded, ignoring James entirely. "Are you jealous or something?"

"Hardly! I just think you're way jumping the gun on this whole thing with Lover Boy."

"I get that," Val said, "and it's getting really, really annoying."

"Come on, Val," James said. "Lisa doesn't mean any harm. She's just teasing."

"Well, I don't like that kind of teasing. And she knows I don't like it."

"Excuse me for caring about you," Lisa said, "and not wanting to see you get hurt."

"Don't watch then," Val snapped. "And for your information, Gavin has been nothing but a gentleman — " *sort of* " — and so far you've been way more hurtful and mean than he has. So why don't you do all of us a favor and mind your own business?"

"Maybe I will," Lisa said, looking hurt.

"It'd be a first," Val said.

"Wow," said James. "That's really cold, Val."

She glared at him, then at Lisa, then turned her back and walked away. One of them called after her but she didn't look around, afraid that they'd see the tears sparkling in her eyes if she did. Keeping her head down, she headed for the nearest restroom.

People were always telling her, "Val, you need to stand up for yourself!" They said that being empowered would make her feel good. And it did, in a way. She had gotten a savage sort of satisfaction from seeing Lisa's eyes open wide like that, with respect — and maybe a little fear.

But mostly, it made Val feel like throwing up.

Fearscape by Nenia Campbell

Chapter Eight

Days passed, and time did nothing to alleviate Val's anger. She had trusted Lisa, tried to get her involved, and she had betrayed her — and for what? A stupid joke? She knew Lindsay and Rachel were curious about Lisa's continued absence from their table, but they never broached the subject. Probably afraid of looking the proverbial gift horse in the mouth, too. Their dislike of Lisa, and their disdain for James, was certainly no secret.

On the days when Rachel and Lindsay had French Club she sat with Gavin in the grassy quad beneath the tree where they had drawn one another — and where he had kissed her for the first time. She sat with him after school, and before Art, too, if they were both early enough.

She kept expecting him to kiss her again, or invite her out, but he didn't. He seemed perfectly content to relax against the trunk of the tree, or even just lie down in the grass, and hold her against him, with his hands clasped slightly over her midriff beneath the hem of her shirt.

Should she ask him out? He certainly wasn't shy and had his own way of doing things, which made her wary. She didn't want him to think her desperate — but she also didn't want him to think that she was content with something purely physical, either.

"You run today, don't you?" His voice was worn velvet in her ear.

"Yes," said Val.

He stroked the side of her leg through his jeans. "I think you need it."

No arguments here, she thought, and sighed, leaning back against him.

"You should come running with me some time," he murmured.

"If you can keep up," Val said, with a lightness that surprised her.

"What I lack in speed, I make up for in endurance."

Val resisted the urge to roll her eyes. Talk like that got you slapped into long-distance running. "Are you in a sport? Do you still do archery?"

"I don't recall telling you about that," he said dryly.

Val's face flushed. "Oh — "

"You've been stalking me," he said, giving her a little

squeeze. "However will I sleep at night?"

"I just used Google," she said hotly. "I would never — "

"Calm down. It's all right. I don't mind you Googling me. In fact, I find the idea very appealing." He looked at her. She was too embarrassed to meet his eyes, let alone respond. Smiling now, he continued, "In response to your question, no. I no longer participate in the school's archery club. I run. I swim. I lift weights. Oh — and play chess, of course."

"The intellectual sport," Val said.

"Yes, quite. Though running is not without its merits. Supposedly, aerobic activity increases the formation of new synapses — and there's you. I bet you look amazing when you run."

And that sent a pang through her —

(Tell me, why is it that you run? Is it to chase? Or to flee?)

"Come watch us sometime."

(I'd give a lot to)

"Perhaps I will."

(know.)

■□■□■□■

Running *was* amazing.

Val admitted this to herself later, on the track field. She loved the way her body felt as she ripped through the air. There were moments, after getting good purchase on the track for a bound, that she almost felt as if invisible wings were unfurling from her back, giving her extra lift.

She couldn't really blame Gavin for his interest, particularly since she had made it so clear that running was important to her. James certainly hadn't. She should be flattered, really.

Curse her stalker.

Curse James.

Curse Lisa.

It had been exactly one week since her fight with Lisa. The blonde girl had been ignoring her, both at school and on Facebook, and had thus far made no attempts at reconciliation. Clearly the expectation was that she, Val, should be the first to wave the olive branch. That was how it had always happened in the past. *Well, not this time.*

She let out her breath. Pain knifed through her side, causing her to falter a little. After an hour of running she was starting to get fatigued. A leaden heaviness had settled in her calves and there was a lump in her throat that refused to yield to her frequent swallows.

With a sigh that was part wheeze, Val jogged to the water fountain. It was a crude spigot, hanging over a wooden trough filled with gravel, but all that mattered was that the water was cold and didn't taste too much like undissolved zinc. She took a long, deep drink, cupping her hands beneath the steady stream of water to splash her sweaty face.

"Val, you're on fire," Lindsay panted. "What's your secret?"

Val lowered her hands, causing the excess water to fall against the gravel with a slap. "Anger," she said, once she'd caught her breath. "Lisa is mad at me for some stupid reason. And I'm mad at her, too. I think."

"You think?" Rachel, who had joined them early enough to hear the start of this conversation, lifted one dark eyebrow. "You mean you aren't sure?"

"No, I'm mad. But I'm also disappointed and kind of sad. We've been friends for a while."

"Hey, if she's willing to throw that away over something that stupid — what got her panties in a twist again, you not wanting to date her precious James?" Rachel snorted. "That says more about her than you. She's not your pimp."

"Yeah, I mean seriously," Lindsay said, swiping her forehead with the back of her terrycloth wristbands. "I never really liked her, though."

"How *are* things with Hi — with that Gavin guy? He still behaving himself?"

Val looked at Rachel sharply but the near-slip appeared to be unintentional. "Things have been okay. He's been, um, very friendly. We talk in Art sometimes."

Though he'd been a little scarce lately.

She didn't have his cell, and he didn't have a Facebook, so she only really talked to him at school. Sometimes he didn't even talk to her in Art at all, and she kept fearing that he, too, would lose interest in her, and end up kicking her to the curb.

The thought made her feel terribly lonely. Without James or Lisa in her life, Val was suddenly, painfully conscious of just how her social circle was.

"Have you kissed him yet?" Lindsay wanted to know.

"Um, well … yes?"

"How was he?" Rachel asked, grinning.

"I don't know." Val turned red. "I've never actually kissed anyone before."

"Aww, are you blushing? You are too cute." Rachel patted her on the head. "Isn't she cute?"

"Very," Lindsay agreed. "Just make sure Gavin keeps his hands to himself when he's not welcome. If he doesn't treat you right," she punched her fist into her palm, "we'll rough him up."

"Good luck with that, Wonder Woman," Rachel said.

A drop of water fell on Val's nose. She winced, thinking it was a bead of sweat. Then another fell as she tilted her head up, right in the eye, and she noticed how the sky was darkening. Clouds as black as blobs of ink were rolling in, blotting out the tentative, greenish light peeking through the cloud cover. A cold wind ringed the three girls and Val went from burning up to freezing.

"God, that's cold." Val rubbed at her bare arms, shivering. "Looks like a big storm."

Lindsay stuck her tongue out at the clouds. "Back in Kansas, a sky like that meant business."

"I didn't know you used to live in Kansas."

"Me, either." Rachel cut her eyes at Lindsay. "Bitch. I thought we were best friends. What else haven't you been telling me?"

"It's not something I like to tell people. It makes people think I'm a hick or that I have inbred cousins." She rolled her eyes. "Like they wouldn't get just as uptight if they were asked about their backyard marijuana gardens and movie star neighbors."

"That's just dumb," said Val.

"I don't think of inbred cousins," Rachel said helpfully. "I think of the Wizard of — "

"Finish that sentence and you're a dead woman," Lindsay said.

"Come on girls." The coach clapped her hands and all three of them looked up. "Locker rooms, stat. We've been rained out."

"Well, you heard the coach. Let's get hopping, Toto. We're not on the track field anymore."

Rachel squealed as Lindsay lunged for her. The two of them zigzagged through the rain, giggling and shouting, as they knotted through their tired teammates.

Fearscape by Nenia Campbell

Val laughed, and then cut off guiltily as if she felt it weren't something she was permitted to do. She eyed the dark clouds looming from behind, and at the shadowy bleachers. It was creepy. She felt watched, but there was nobody there. None that she could see, anyway.

I wonder.

But when she got to her locker it was clean. No flowers. No poetry. No writing.

She let out a quiet sigh of relief and slung her backpack over her shoulder. There was no point in changing into her regular clothes, she thought. They'd just get soaked — and she was already sweaty. She pulled out her phone from her track jacket and dialed home but no one answered.

Did her mother have something going on today? No, she hadn't given Val bus fare.

"Come on," she said, dialing again. "Mom, what the hell? Pick up the phone."

But the busy signal was obstinate.

"Damn it." Val plopped down on the school's rain-slicked front steps with her wet hair hanging in her eyes. *Now what am I supposed to do?* She started to call Lindsay, hoping her friend hadn't already gotten too far from campus, when a white Camaro rolled up to the curb.

The window cranked down, and a familiar voice said, "Val?"

She jumped up, raking her hair out of her face. "Gavin? Where did you come from?"

"The art building. I was helping Ms. Wilcox with things." He trailed off. "Are you waiting for someone?"

"My mom. I'm going to be running a fever if she doesn't get here soon."

"Is she on her way?"

"No," Val said. "I can't get hold of her."

"I could give you a ride," he said carefully.

She felt a bolt of dread and something else, something like anticipation. "I live on the other side of town from here. I'm probably way out of your way."

"You are, but you can wait at my house, if you like. Surely you have someone else that you can call to pick you up." When she hesitated, his smile morphed into a grin. "I don't bite, Val. Not hard. Not unless I'm asked to."

The rain did nothing to cool her face. "Okay," she

mumbled.

"Get in." He reached over and popped the lock for her — a manual lock. God, this car was old. She opened the door and slid into the seat, aware that she was dripping water all over the upholstery and floor. "I'm getting water everywhere — "

"It's nothing." He turned up the heater.

The inside of the car was clean and warm, smelling of leather, and coffee, and aftershave. Val relaxed a little at the soothing blend of scents and tugged off her jacket, holding it in front of the hot air blasting from his dashboard. Her skin felt clammy and dead where it had been in contact with the wet fabric. She shivered again, and caught him glancing at her uniform.

She hugged her backpack to her chest. "Thanks again."

"It's nothing," he said.

The silence made her uncomfortable. He didn't listen to music and except for the patter of rain and the roar of the heater, it was silent.

"I hope this isn't weird," she blurted.

"Weird?" His eyes flicked towards her and returned to the road.

"You still don't know anything about me. For all you know, I could be a psychopath."

He smiled at that, but kept his eyes straight ahead. "I'll take my chances."

"I could even be a serial killer," she went on, emboldened, wanting to make him laugh.

He did.

Gavin lived near the hills, in the foothills practically, in one of the larger houses. He pressed a button on his keys and the garage door swung open. As he maneuvered the car inside she couldn't help noticing how empty it was. Her father would have killed for such Spartan neatness.

"It's so clean," she said, doing a little spin. "Did your dad do this?"

Oh, wait. He didn't have a dad, she remembered. Or at least, not a listed one. She nearly apologized and then remembered that she wasn't supposed to know that.

"I did it myself," he said, "thanks. It's convenient, parking inside. No need to get wet."

She nodded, and slung her jacket over her arm. *Idiot*, she chastened. *He hates you.*

Gavin opened the door leading into the house. The rooms were big, but bereft. She stared at what she supposed was the living room, devoid of anything but two chairs, a bookshelf, a love seat, and a chess table. "Your family's not too big on TV, huh?" she said.

"I live alone."

"Oh." She blinked as the implications of those words sank in. "Oh, God — I'm so sorry!"

"They're not dead. I just don't live with them. I haven't for a while, now. Not since I was sixteen."

It took Val a moment to speak. "I thought you had to be eighteen to — "

"Live alone?" he finished. "Technically, you do. But there are always exceptions. You'll learn that soon enough. Go ahead and sit down. I'm going to make some tea. It's cold in here."

Val sat in the chair closest to the chess set and tried her phone again. The line was still busy. She set it on the edge of the table, shaking her head. Living alone since age sixteen? She couldn't imagine. That sounded so lonely. No wonder he was so strange! Her parents weren't perfect, but she wouldn't even know where to begin without them.

(his family is crazy)

Had he been one of those — what was the phrase? — emancipated minors?

Gavin walked back into the room and handed her a steaming cup of tea, setting his own down at the table before taking the chair across from hers. His eyes skipped from the board to her face. "Do you play?" he asked, taking a sip of tea.

The fumes from hers were heady and sweet. Mint, she thought. "No."

He set the cup down. "I can teach you. Would you like to learn?"

Val stared at the small army of pieces. There were so many. "If you want to teach me."

"It would be a pleasure, Val. Really, the game is quite simple once you understand how they move. The short, round ones are pawns — " he picked up one of the stunted chessmen comprising the first rank " — they can only move one space forward at a time and always capture diagonally. Except for the first move, where they have the choice of moving two spaces — and for *en passant*, where a pawn can capture another pawn that has also moved ahead two."

"Pawn passant," Val said.

"Quite. Chess pieces are rather territorial, but we won't be worrying about that for now," he added, glimpsing her confusion. "The ones that look like stallions are called knights and they move, and capture, in an L-shaped pattern, three by one spaces in any direction you desire.

"The pointed ones are bishops. They move, and capture, diagonally. The castles are called rooks and can move horizontally or vertically. They can also be used in a defensive move called castling in tandem with the king. We'll get to him in a moment after we discuss his lovely consort."

"Consort?" Val repeated blankly.

He picked up the black queen. "Yes. Consort. The queen is arguably the most powerful piece in the game. She can move like a rook and a bishop combined, carving out large sections of the board for herself and placing them under her power."

Val watched him set the piece down. "What can the king do?"

Gavin's lip curled. "Not much, I'm afraid. Like the queen, he can move in any direction but his scope is limited to one space only. He's rather like a glorified pawn."

"Oh," said Val.

"Yes, well — " he tapped the board, " — shall we?"

Val played White. She didn't want to, but he insisted, and she immediately proceeded to fumble the game. Several times, she moved pieces the wrong way, and when she tried to castle she switched the rook with the queen instead. Each time, though, he corrected her mistakes with impassivity, and when she realized he wasn't going to laugh at her she began to enjoy herself.

In many ways, chess was similar to the video games she played on her various consoles at home. There were rules, and you could not bend them. Sometimes you could work them in conjunction with one another, though, and play the field to your advantage — but there were no cheat codes for extra chessmen or power-ups in chess.

Gavin might as well have been cheating, though. He was good. Very good. Incredibly good. Even as a beginner, she could tell. He spun complex traps, so many moves in advance that, in retrospect, the innocuous move of a pawn suddenly seemed like a harbinger of doom.

Fearscape by Nenia Campbell

Before ten moves were up, she was already down as many pieces.

"Running away from me?" he teased, when she was forced to retreat. "So soon?"

"You're going to win," she protested.

"Oh, I think I've already won, my dear." He'd infiltrated the ranks of her pieces and took one of her rooks, simultaneously making sure that she couldn't castle with the other. "I'm just playing with you now." He studied the rook in his hand for a moment before placing it off to the side.

"Why would you do that? It's not very nice."

"Don't make it so easy for me to take advantage of you, then." He took another piece.

She glared at him.

Levelly, he returned her gaze, his lips curved like a cat's. "What would you say if I told you that I could have checkmated you and ended the game ten turns ago?"

"I'd say you're messing with me."

"Perhaps. Perhaps not. How sure are you? Sure enough to make a bet?"

The intent look in his eyes made her falter. "What kind of

bet?"

"How confident do you feel?"

"P-pretty confident."

"Really?"

"Yes?"

"Well, in that case … you would be wrong."

"What?" Her eyes scanned the board. "I don't see ho — "

He moved his knight, which had been in the corner this whole time, forgotten and harmless. Or so she'd thought.

"Checkmate." He picked up his tea and sipped it as she stared at the board. "Good thing were weren't playing for keeps, isn't it?"

She must have looked startled, because he set down his cup and said, "Good game." When he clasped her hand in his it was warm, almost hot, from the mug of tea he'd been holding. "You put up a good fight," and his grip tightened briefly before he pulled away, "trust me; I've played with some of the best — I know."

"What was that like?"

"Exhilarating." She watched his eyes go to the window. The sky had grown less menacing and Val could make out the faded twilight peering through the gaps in the denim-dark clouds. "You should call home, perhaps," he added, as if as an afterthought.

Val glanced at her phone, did a double-take. *Oh my god, it's 7:13.* Her mother would be worried sick. She probably already was. How had so much time elapsed without her noticing? She hazarded a look at Gavin, now cleaning up the board, and answered her own question.

Her legs shook a little when she got up from the chair, after sitting still for so long. She dialed her home number. The phone picked up on the first ring. "Hello?" Her mother's voice was wary.

"Um, Mom? It's me, Val — I'm done with track practice."

"Val? What happened? Are you all right? I was so worried. I tried to call you nearly half a dozen times but you didn't answer."

Val glanced at her call history. "I never got any calls from you, and my phone was on the entire time."

"It must have been the storm," Val's mother said, "it took out one of the telephone poles and caused a power surge several blocks over — you weren't outside, were you? Where are you now? Still at school?"

"N-no! Don't worry. I stayed at an, um — " Gavin was still setting up the pieces, not looking at her, but that didn't mean he wasn't listening. "At a friend's," she finished, turning back around and perching herself on the arm of the leather chair, subsequently missing the satisfied smirk that marred his face at her words.

"Lisa's?"

"No."

"Someone from track?"

"Mom, I have friends outside track." She gave her mother the address, adding, "It's pretty to find. He lives in the big house with the white shutters at the end of the street."

A pause. "He?"

Uh-oh.

"Is this the boy you were telling me about in the car? The senior?"

She made the word sound tantamount to 'senior citizen.' "It's not like that. He just — "

"This is neither the time nor the place to discuss it. You, your father, and I shall be talking about this later, young lady."

"But I didn't — "

"I'm on my way now. I'll be there in fifteen minutes. Be ready."

The phone went dead. Val glared at it.

"Is there a problem?"

"No." Val buried her face in her hands. "Oh, maybe. I don't know."

"I hope it wasn't through any oversight of mine."

Val wasn't entirely sure what 'oversight' meant. "My mom's — " *stupid* " — protective."

"Ah, I see. So she thought that you, and I— " he was standing in front of her now, she hadn't even heard him move " — were playing a different kind of game. Is that the gist of it?"

Val swallowed nervously. "That's, um … yeah. About the gist of it."

"Because I'll admit the thought has crossed my mind." He took another step closer, so that he was standing between her dangling legs. "On occasion." The caress of his still-warm hands at her waist and the intimacy of the skin-on-skin contact made her jump; despite their warmth, his fingers seemed to leave strings of rime in their wake. "Now."

The desperate wanting in his eyes scared her. She felt like she was teetering on the edge of a yawning abyss, one misstep away from falling headlong into dark waters. And when she did, she wondered, would she float — or would she drown? She was certainly drowning now; she could barely breathe.

"You're so beautiful, you know. I've always thought so. Wild and artless."

Really? She didn't think those words described her — not at all. *He's going to kiss me*, Val thought, watching him watch her and quelling an irrational urge to flee. *I really think he is.*

If this was love, it felt different than she'd imagined it would, walking a thin line between passion and terror. It was Romeo and Juliet. It was Wuthering Heights. And Val was left petrified from the boiling intensity of it. "I'm just ordinary me." She wet her lips. "I'm nothing special. Not like that."

His eyes dropped to her mouth. "Show me," he said, and with a clash of teeth and lips, they were kissing, and the rain on her skin seemed to blaze. He placed her hands, which were pressed against his chest as if trying to push him away, around his neck, pulling her closer. His own hands returned to settle at her waist, tracing spirals, swirls: scratching runes of fire into her skin.

The lump of ice in her throat seemed to melt, trickling into her belly and simmering like hot honey, filling her lungs with dizzying steam that suffocated even as it intoxicated. His lips disappeared from hers and she felt the scrape of his stubbly cheek against her neck and the sandpaper roughness of his tongue as he kissed the place where her heart beat fastest.

Her breathing quickened and she felt faint, like a rabbit not sure whether to freeze or bolt. He bit her and she felt his tongue trail over her skin, tasting the marks he'd left, before returning to her mouth.

"I like the way your hands feel on me."

A shiver arced down her spine, white and electric with guilt. Her fingers were curled in his hair, which had the texture of fur. She dropped her hands from his head as if she'd been burned — and in a way, she had been. She couldn't remember laying her hands on him like that. It was too rough, too proprietary, too ….

Too him.

Yes. Proprietary. That was the word. He acted like he owned her. She didn't like that.

Did she?

His lips brushed the neckline of her shirt and he gave it an impatient tug with his teeth, she nearly lost her balance. If he hadn't been holding her she would have tumbled head-first over the arm of the chair, and that still seemed less dangerous than staying in his embrace a moment longer. "Stop," she said, "please. My mother's coming, and I don't — "

"Want her seeing her little Red consorting with the wolf?"

Val was disturbed. "Don't say things like that. I don't like it when you say things like that."

"I wanted you to see, if only for a moment, what I see when I look at you." She shivered when he took a step back, because for a moment she'd feared he wasn't going to, and a rush of cold air filled the space where his body heat had previously warmed her. He was still holding onto her, though at a distance now, and after a moment's pause, even this bit of vestigial contact ceased. "You might say that you bring out the animal in me," he said, and chuckled.

The room seemed to be spinning slightly. "You're not a

wolf."

"A wolf hunts on instinct, without compunction. So do I. For the very same reasons, I could ask you why you run. You're not a deer — and yet you use the same instincts as a creature under pursuit."

Her skin prickled. "That's nowhere even close to being about the same thing."

"Oh, but it is. Because I bring out the animal in you, too, I think." He ran his knuckles along her neck, ghosting the trail his mouth had blazed only minutes before. "Hmm. You're going to have a mark there. Redheads bruise so easily…"

She pulled her head back. "Do you ever watch me? I mean out on the track, when I run."

"Have you ever seen me watching you?"

"That doesn't answer my question." She grabbed her jacket, zipped it up to the throat. "I'm being serious."

"So was I." The doorbell rang. "I'll get it," he said, giving her a knowing smile. "My dear."

My dear? Or 'my deer?'

She wondered how he could sound so composed when her knees were a step from giving out.

Chapter Nine

"Arctic" would have been an apt word to describe the car ride home. Val sat in the back seat, the stiff heads of her parents as formidable as stone statues in the front seats of the car. She closed her eyes and leaned back against her headrest, trying to blot out the icy, awkward silence. Trying to make sense of her own inner chaos — that kiss — his confusing and frightening words —

Gavin had given her mother a reception worthy of the queen, introducing himself, offering her tea, coffee, even managing to drop a courtly bow that, while not mitigating Mrs. Kimble's anger in the slightest, elicited a raised eyebrow and twitching lip.

After a polite refusal she said, coldly, "Come, Val."

Sulkily, she went, humiliated that her mother would do this in front of a boy. But not so humiliated that she couldn't look back. And when she did, she saw that he was watching her, too. And in that instant before the door closed behind him with a neat click, she thought he winked.

As soon as they pulled into the driveway, Val hopped out of the van and let herself into the house with her own key. She took the steps two at a time, stomping a little as she did. Her thoughts were scrambled, frenetic, but nowhere near as bad in shape as her emotions. She tore off her wet track clothes, throwing them to the side with a vengeance that surprised her. When she pulled on her sweats, the warm fleece felt strange against her cold, clammy skin, and made her shiver all the harder.

Knocking sounded upon her door. "Val, it's your father. Your mother is waiting in the kitchen. She wants to speak with you alone."

A pause.

"*Now*, Val."

Crap.

She walked into the brightly lit kitchen filled with apprehension. Her mother had changed into her pajamas and the purple-checked nightgown made her look very thin and frail. Unlike Val, Mrs. Kimble was blonde, and her thin skin had developed the texture and consistency of tissue paper from too much tanning and smoking as a teen.

At the sound of Val's footsteps, her mother looked up. The muscles in her cheeks and under her eyes were strained. She didn't beat around the bush. She said, "What could have possessed you to make you think that was a good idea?"

Val sat on the edge of the kitchen chair farthest from her mother. "The line was busy."

"And you couldn't have waited at school?"

"It was raining — and cold."

"So you got into a strange car with a strange man — "

"He goes to my school!"

" — and went to his house, drinking whatever he gave you — "

"Tea," Val cut in. "It was just tea!"

"And what if it had been drugged?" Her mother asked. "What then?"

He wouldn't do that. He'd want me awake.

The thought, which had come to her mind unbidden, frightened her.

"Can you at least see why your father and I were so worried? I didn't know where you were. He didn't know where you were. That boy might have taken you anywhere. He might have — " Her mouth tightened, and she was unable to finish the thought. Wrapped around her mug of tea, her knuckles whitened, though, and, seeing her daughter's gaze, she set it down gently on the table. "I worry about you," she said. "You're so young."

Val allowed herself to be hugged. She sensed a peaceful resolution. "Gavin wouldn't do anything like that," she said, doubting the words even as they left her mouth. Because she wondered now. She wondered.

"I'll admit that his manners were nice, at the very least," her mother said grudgingly. "He's a very polite boy, very formal, but that says nothing about what he's like as a person."

"Ms. Wilcox likes him."

"Some of the cruelest men in the world were born with silver tongues. They could charm a bird right out of the sky, only to break its wings. And no men, nice or cruel, offer favors lightly — not strangers. Not to young women. Not without expecting something back in return."

The look in her mother's eyes made Val squirm. "We're just classmates."

"Is that his opinion? Or yours?"

"It's the truth."

"You're blushing," Mrs. Kimble said. "That leads me to suspect otherwise."

At Val's silence, she sighed.

"All right. Then go to your room."

The next afternoon he was stretched out in their usual spot, lying in the grass with no regard for his white sweater. There were two coffees beside him. "What's this?" she asked, surprised.

"It was the least I could do." He smiled up at her. "I hope they weren't too hard on you."

"Not too hard," Val mumbled, feeling a little like a parrot. She dropped to the grass.

"Was that your mother?"

"Yeah," Val said. She sipped at the coffee he'd given her. Hazelnut. Had she told him that she liked hazelnut? She couldn't remember, but she didn't think so.

"You look nothing like her."

"I look like my great-aunt Agnes," Val said. "On my father's side. Can I ask you a question?"

"You just did," he said lazily.

Val wasn't in the mood for games. "Why do you bother with me?"

Gavin rolled onto his side to regard her. "Because I like being bothered," he said. "By you."

"No, I mean — " Val fumbled for the words to explain her amorphous doubts. They were many, and vague. " — why me?" she decided upon at last. "What do you see in me?"

"Ah. That's different." He ran his fingers along the necklace at his throat, following the chain to the clasp at the back. With a sigh, he unfastened it and let the metal links coil around his fingers like a serpent. "What brought this on?"

"I'm just curious."

"A very dangerous thing, that."

"Why?"

"Because," he let the necklace slip from his fingers to swing like a pendulum, "it leads people to answers that they might not necessarily like. Possibility — that's what I see in you. Among other things."

Her eyes, which had been following the chain's hypnotic arc, came to an abrupt standstill on his face. "Possibility for what?"

"Me."

"I don't understand."

"I'm very particular. In all things — but women, especially. There are traits I absolutely require, and you, my dear, possess many of them. Suffice it to say I am very interested. Nobody has ever managed to capture and hold my attention as you have."

"Like what?" Val persisted. "What traits?"

Gavin sat up. "Beauty. Innocence." He drew her closer. "Submissiveness."

"What about intelligence?"

"Oh, yes. That's a necessity."

"Kindness? Compassion?"

"You could do without quite so much of that." He paused. "Curiosity. That's one I rather like."

"You just said curiosity was dangerous."

"I enjoy a bit of danger, too," he whispered, and she felt the cold bite of metal against her skin. She looked down just in time to see him fasten the clasp of the necklace around her wrists.

"What are you doing?"

Fearscape by Nenia Campbell

"Don't you trust me, Val?" His voice, soft as death in her ear. She shivered.

No. She didn't. Not at all. That realization thrilled and frightened her as he got to his feet and walked away. *What is he doing? Where is he going?* She heard the grass rustle as he circled around behind her. Val tried to look over her shoulder and his hand covered her eyes. She jerked. "What are you — "

"Shh. I'm going to tell you a secret." His lips brushed against her ear, causing ripples of sensation down that side of her face, and Val found herself shying away from the sheer intimacy of it. "Can you keep a secret?"

Torn, she said, "Yes, but — "

"I sometimes think I'm more beast than man."

Val stiffened. "That's silly."

"Is it? We all started out in the wilds. It stands to reason that some of us would retain that more than others. Humanity is a cage, and our puritanical sensibilities comprise the bars. We are confined by our own reason and intellect, and yet most of us don't even know it."

"That's a horrible thing to say. Untie me," she protested. "I don't like this."

"No, you wouldn't, would you?" he breathed. "You're like a half-tamed creature, still shy of the bridle. 'Except you enthrall me, never shall be free.' But freedom is an illusion, anyway."

Those words …. "Donne," she choked.

"Mm-hmm. And — 'Love will find a way through paths where wolves fear to prey.'" His lips brushed the hollow beneath her ear. "That's Byron. A libertine, and rather eloquent for one so crude and base. But then, beauty so often can be found in the very depths of degradation." In a different sort of voice, he said, lowly, "What time did you tell your mother you'd be home?"

"Now. Let me go right now."

"Am I making you uncomfortable?"

Yes.

She felt his finger slide along the space between her skin and the chain. "Or could it be that you're afraid someone might see you like this, with me?"

That possibility hadn't even occurred to her until now. "Oh, god," she whispered. He let her struggle, with an air of superior indulgence which frightened her. Then, just when she was about to cry, he reached around her body to unfasten the clasp. She wasted no time in backing away from him, her heart pounding, her palms sweating.

"Don't be angry with me." She flinched when he reached out to pat her cheek. "I couldn't resist teasing you."

He sounded contrite, but the look in his eyes — it was all wrong.

"I have to go," she said stiffly.

"You're angry."

His eyes are empty.

"And frightened."

There's nothing in there. Nothing but shadows.

"I'm not," she said, and it sounded as unconvincing aloud as it did in her head.

"I'll drive you home," he said.

And since Val couldn't think of a polite way to refuse without being circumspect, she let him. The drive spanned in silence, crackling with a tension that bordered on electric. Though Gavin kept his eyes on the road she had the feeling that none of her movements escaped his notice.

His words curled in her ears like steam, even now, as dark

as the fears in her secret heart.

(I sometimes think I'm more beast than man)

■□■□■□■

Gavin dropped her off at her home with a lingering kiss that made her lips feel numb. She mumbled an intelligible farewell and ran inside the house, locking the door behind her. Her heart was hammering, and she could still feel the sting of his necklace on her wrists: cold metal warmed by human skin.

Val dumped her backpack on her bed, unzipping it roughly. She grabbed the first notebook she touched, her Health binder, and a green gel-pen with only about a quarter of its ink remaining.

On an empty sheet, she slashed a green line, dividing the paper into two columns. One she labeled *Gavin*, the other labeled *Stalker*. In her tiniest handwriting, she wrote down everything she knew about both individuals and didn't stop until she drew a blank.

The similarities between the two were terrifying.

But what did that mean for her? The man who had sent her those messages scared her on a deep and profound level. Because Val suspected that he didn't consider her a person at all, but an animal — no, worse still: something to be owned, played with, trifled with, and then discarded once broken.

Ever since the first message, Val had started getting nightmares about getting caught alone, in the dark. She wasn't sure what a man like that might do to her, but she knew enough to know she wouldn't like it.

That actually spoke in Gavin's favor, though, because so far he had done nothing to hurt her. Not really. And she was attracted to him, too. When he had kissed her, the ground seemed to have fallen right out from beneath her feet.

On the other hand, Gavin had known her mother was expecting her home by a set time, both times.

What would he have done if she hadn't been expected back for a while longer? Would he still have let her go?

Everything was connecting with far more ease than she would have liked. *I shouldn't even be thinking like this. I'm freaking myself out.*

Every time she closed her eyes, she felt his breath on her neck, that firm, insistent pressure on her lips — and that vague impression that he was hunting her, like a deer in the woods. A dark huntsman.

Mr. and Mrs. Kimble had gone out for dinner, leaving her to stew like meat in a crock pot. Val had begged them to take her with them, as if she were four instead of fourteen, not wanting to be left alone in their large house with far too many doors and windows.

Her father had rolled his eyes. "Very funny, Val."

Her mother had seemed to know Val wasn't joking, but she, too, said no. "The reservations are for two, not three," she explained, "and it's so crowded during dinner hour that they most likely won't be able to scrounge up another chair. And besides, I'm sure you don't want to be stuck with your lovey-dovey parents."

Anything would be better than this isolation.

So she locked all the doors and closed all the blinds. A knife from the kitchen was beside her on the desk. Her mother wouldn't miss it — it was the one with the loose blade and the scratched-up handle; the one nobody used.

Val knew she had to come up with a plan to find the truth behind all of this because at the moment, she could only suspect. And while she was afraid of being wrong, she was even more afraid of being right. Gavin knew who her friends were, where she lived, what her habits and hobbies were. If he was her stalker, he possessed more than enough information to be a major threat. And how many high school students could there be, talking as if they were from *Wuthering Heights?*

Plus, he had quoted that poem to her, the one by John Donne. The way he had spoken, it was almost as if he wanted some sort of reaction. Like recognition.

There had to be some clues *somewhere.*

His house, perhaps?

She could tell him she wanted another chess lesson, and then find an excuse to snoop around. To be really safe, she could even bring the knife. But that would imply that she was prepared to use it, and Val had never hurt a soul in her life ….

Chapter Ten

The next day was a Saturday.

Val lay on her bed, motionless, watching the branches of the trees cast shadows upon the walls of her room that resembled an undulating spiderweb. On her nightstand were the knife, the flashlight, two energy drinks, and a Nancy Drew mystery.

Not that she believed that her stalker would come for her in her own home. Not really. But each creak and groan of the settling house made Val freeze and hold her breath. It wasn't until her parents came through the door, giggling and slightly tipsy, that Val switched off the flashlight and let her exhausted body cut loose.

And then, the nightmares came.

"Val?" Someone rapped lightly on her door. "Valerian?"

She didn't respond. Just closed her eyes. *It's daylight now. I'm safe — let me rest.*

The door creaked open. Her mother's concerned face peered through the gap. "Val, are you — oh. You were so quiet, I thought you were still asleep. Aren't you coming downstairs?"

Fearscape by Nenia Campbell

"No."

"But I made breakfast."

"I'm not hungry. I don't want to eat."

"Honey, you haven't been down all day." With the way Mrs. Kimble was glancing around her bedroom, as though looking for signs of drugs or debauchery, Val was glad she'd remembered to push the knife behind her nightstand before going to sleep. "Are you all right?"

"I'll eat later."

"That doesn't answer my question. Are you sick?" Her mother's cool hand pressed against Val's forehead. "You're a little warm."

"I'm just tired."

"Do I need to take you to the doctor?"

"No." The doctor wouldn't find what was wrong with her. Not unless he cut open her head and her veins, to see how corroded Gavin had rendered her thoughts and blood, respectively.

"Can I bring you anything?"

"Maybe soup — and tea."

Her mother's frown deepened. "Yes, I can do that. What

kind?"

"Chamomile and chicken noodle … please."

"All right. I'll bring some up on a tray." With a final look, Mrs. Kimble left.

Val reached down beside her bed and pulled her laptop onto her quilt. She logged into Facebook. There were four new messages. Knowing it was a bad idea, but being unable to help herself, she clicked the red flag.

One was from Lisa and consisted of one word: Hey.

Another was from Rachel:

You looked a little peaky on Friday. Are you okay? It's not that guy, right? Just let us know whose ass to kick and we'll take care of it.

Sorry, that was Lindsay. But seriously, are you all right? Text us.

xox

The other two were from her stalker. One from last night:

Soon, my dear, you will learn to love your imprisonment.

And the other from this morning:

Can you feel the ties that bind us? Can you feel them tightening? Because I can, and they're so tight that I can scarcely breathe.

That made two of them.

■□■□■□■

The next day was a Sunday.

There were no Facebook messages that morning, but out of sight did not necessarily mean out of mind. Not when he was thinking about her, counting down the days until he would own her.

Her mother barged into Val's room as per her usual wake-up call and decided to put an end to the lounging around in bed. "Get dressed," she said, in a tone that brooked no argument. "You're running errands with me. Be ready in ten."

"Okay," said a meek Val.

Mrs. Kimble deposited Val at a nearby Starbucks while she went to pick up groceries, leaving her daughter with explicit orders to "have fun." Val stared bleakly at the menu and ended up ordering a tall vanilla bean frappuccino — but it was sweeter than she expected, and she didn't have the heart to finish it.

While her drink melted, and Nat King Cole crooned through the speakers about heartbreak, Val pulled her Health notebook from her bag and studied the list she'd drawn up several days ago. It seemed stupid now, foolish, tantamount to a child's black-and-white logic. Breaking into his house? A violent confrontation? In what world was that actually a good idea?

Val took a sip of her drink and winced. In addition to being too sweet, it was now watery. The next day would be a Monday. If she didn't make a move now, it might be too late. If Gavin was her stalker, she wanted to know. She didn't want to be captured. She didn't want to play the lead role in his twisted fantasies. She wanted to be — well, she wasn't sure yet, but not this.

When her mother returned to collect her she was disappointed to find her daughter just as morose as before, accompanied by an expensive — and very melted — drink. She nearly asked Val what was wrong, but had recently read an article online saying that children, when pressed, only dove deeper into their funk out of spite.

Not that Mrs. Kimble thought of Val as a spiteful child. Quite the opposite. She was a very sweet girl — a little too sweet, actually, like the drink she was holding in her hand

Fearscape by Nenia Campbell

(Mrs. Kimble tried a sip before throwing it away, and imagined that she could feel her fillings loosening already. She would have to remind Val to brush her teeth twice). When Val was a child, and the other kids on the playground sometimes hit her with a shovel or a pail, she never hit them back. She just cried, as if the belief that someone could actually want to hurt her was too horrible to bear.

It had always been this way. Val was delicate. Smart and sweet and beautiful, but delicate as a hothouse flower. And despite being grateful for her charmingly naïve daughter, who as a young woman looked upon the world rather as a child did, she sometimes wished that Val was a little more robust and, though she felt evil for thinking this, a little less pretty. People only picked the pretty, sweet-smelling flowers. The ones with thorns were left alone.

A screech of tires made Mrs. Kimble slam on the brakes. "Oh my God, Val, that boy just cut me off — at a red light." She blasted the horn at the driver. "The light was *red*!"

For her efforts, Mrs. Kimble received an upraised middle finger.

Such disrespect! Val's mother squawked in outrage.

Noting the Derringer High School bumper sticker, Mrs. Kimble said, in scathing tones, "Do you know that boy?"

Val thought Lisa might have dated him a couple times. The beat-up Toyota pickup, with the poorly done paint-job in kelly green was fairly recognizable. But Lisa had maybe-dated a lot of people and Val had eventually lost count. She shook her head. Her mother didn't need to know any of this. There were so many things her mother did not need to know lately.

"I thank my lucky stars every day that *you're* not like that." The cognitive dissonance between her statement and her earlier thoughts made Mrs. Kimble feel guilty, more so when Val kept her eyes trained on the window and stared beyond the glass at something so far off in the distance that her mother was left with the distinct impression that she was never going to catch up.

After a pause, she said, "Did you have fun?" Trying not to look at the melted drink.

"Yes."

"I'm glad."

And each knew that the other was lying, but neither had the faintest idea why.

Fearscape by Nenia Campbell

■□■□■□■

The next day was a Monday.

Val hoped to get the situation she had been dreading all weekend over with right away but fate, it appeared, was conspiring against her. For once, Gavin was late and James took the empty seat beside her that he usually occupied. "Hey, Val. Haven't seen you around lately."

Of course he'd 'seen her around.' They had art together, didn't they? She pulled her sketchpad out of her back pack and made a noncommittal sound.

"So — you and Gavin are going out now, huh?"

Val shrugged. "I don't know."

James's eyes narrowed. "What do you mean, you don't know? You either are or aren't."

Ms. Wilcox saved her from having to respond by choosing that moment to walk into the classroom. She was wearing a purple gypsy dress, a chiffon scarf, and a smile that was considerably warmer than most members of the class warranted.

"Well! Good morning Val, James. Did you have a nice weekend?"

James, pleased to have an active listener in his midst, talked about football and a trip to the beach. His bright, overly loud voice sliced into Val's ears like knives.

"What about you, Val?" their teacher said. She was setting up the day's model — a plastic playset in the shape of a castle, creamy off-white, peppered with glitter, and transparent blue sections that looked as if they could be illuminated from within by LEDs. Ms. Wilcox flipped a switch and it glowed. She turned off the lights and smiled at Val. "Did you do anything nice?"

"I went out with my mom," said Val, briefly. But since she smiled as she said it, Ms. Wilcox found herself thinking, *What a sweet, shy girl she is*. And then other students trickled into the classroom and any other thoughts or concerns Ms. Wilcox had about Val were quickly eclipsed by thoughts and concerns about the other thirty-one students who comprised her class.

She had noticed, however, the relationship budding between Val and her TA. She had seem them out in the quad together, before or after school. Ms. Wilcox liked Gavin. He was polite, solicitous, and saved her a lot of work grading as many papers as he did. But there was something a little chilly in the boy's smile and she worried he might be too "fast" for a girl so shy.

But that was, again, none of her business — and she had thirty-two students to content herself with, besides. If the girl's mother hadn't called to complain, she must have seen no problems with the relationship and it was not Ms. Wilcox's place to get between parent and child. Not when there were students sneaking cigarettes in the backroom, or making off with expensive oil pants she was forced to keep under lock and key. Their parents did call in to complain.

James had watched Ms. Wilcox's departure and waited until she was out of earshot before turning to Val and saying, "You and Lisa okay now?"

With a flash of guilt, Val realized that she'd never bothered to respond to Lindsay, Rachel, *or* Lisa. She bit her lip, shrugged, and said, "I don't know. Ask her."

"I did. She said to ask you."

"Why me?"

"Because you're the one who's still mad."

For God's sake. "I'm not — "

The classroom door opened and Gavin walked in. His

skin was a touch paler than usual and the dark shadows under his eyes hinted at multiple sleepless nights. He glanced in her direction, then at James, and the most terrible expression crossed his face as he turned and sat on the other side of the room, next to a girl who looked very discomfited by his feral appearance.

" — mad," Val finished belatedly. *Oh god.*

"What do you see in the guy?" James persisted.

Val couldn't answer. Because she realized she didn't know herself. And having been given a taste of the thoughts that lay behind that completely intelligible facade, this sent a chill shooting down her spine, as cold and as tangible as a cupful of ice water being poured down her back. Val locked her shoulders and refused to shudder.

"Val?"

She chewed on her lip some more and returned to the castle that was slowly emerging from her sketchpad. The coppery taste of blood filled her mouth, thick and viscous and reminiscent of old pennies. Her stomach rebelled and she only just managed to say, "I don't know."

Did Gavin drink that blood at the pet store?

Fearscape by Nenia Campbell

Is there something wrong with him?

Am I in danger?

"Lisa's very worried about you. She told me to tell you that."

Val looked up. "Why didn't she tell me herself?"

"She's tried. But you haven't exactly been around lately." And his eyes went across the room.

Oh.

Val could feel the weight of Gavin's gaze, hot and unwavering as the dry heat of an oven. James had a point. Maybe. She worked on the castle's outline, sketching the turrets, the complex design of the portcullis, and avoided looking at both boys. *No, he's right.*

James gave her a disappointed look, but at her pointed silence he left her alone and when the bell rang he left without saying goodbye. She had never put much stock in James's opinion, so she wondered that his silent disapprobation could elicit such a wave of guilt inside her now.

Ms. Wilcox clucked over James's messy work station, but she smiled at Val's picture. "Good use of perspective."

"Thanks, Ms. Wilcox." A smile, but unmistakable flush of

pleasure rose in her cheeks, overriding for the moment the feelings of despair and guilt and anxiety that blended to form a spectrum of hazy emotions from her own internal palette. "I used to have a playset like this, I think, when I was a little girl."

Ms. Wilcox smiled again; it was a sad smile. "This was my little girl's. She grew up, too."

For a moment the same unspoken thought hung suspended between them, like a bead of water clinging tenuously on to an edge. *Things are so much easier when you're young.* Then Ms. Wilcox gave a flippant little shrug and began to straighten up the messy desks.

If only Val could shake off her own feelings so easily.

Gavin seized that moment to approach, his footsteps firm and sure. *As if,* she couldn't help thinking, *in his mind he already owns me.* "Good morning," he said, and he leaned over the desk and kissed her, causing her eyes to open wide. She glanced at Ms. Wilcox, but she hadn't seen.

"I — um, hi," she said, and could have kicked herself. She sounded like she'd overdosed on helium. "What do you want?"

"Only to say hello." He paused, "I hope you're well."

Val blanched. "Yes, I'm fine."

"Good. You've been acting so strange lately. I've been concerned."

Threat lanced through his words, but to whom? And about what? Or was she imagining it?

"I'm fine," she said again.

Gavin nodded thoughtfully, turning away. *No, I didn't imagine it.* Val, on her feet by now, hurried after him. "Wait!"

He turned. "Yes, Val?"

Her name from his lips was like a piece of velvet being pulled through a shredder. "Remember when you drove me home that one time in the rain? And taught me how to play chess?"

"That happened recently." Something in his eyes snapped into focus. "How could I forget?"

Val swallowed. Or tried to. A persistent lump kept rising in her throat. *His eyes,* she found herself thinking again. His eyes were beautiful: textured, metallic gray with bubbles of onyx and crystal caught in the twin pools of his irises — but they were shallow, empty, cold, and nothing, not even the thick lashes which framed them, could soften the arctic chill in that gaze. "I was wondering if maybe — do you think you could teach me more?"

He smiled, and she wanted to run. It was the smile of one who had eaten cat, cream, and canary alike. "It would be my distinct pleasure. You can come tomorrow, if you like, or after my shift tonight — I get off at seven."

"Tomorrow is fine," she made herself say.

"Tomorrow it is then. Shall I pick you up at home? Around, oh, shall we say five?"

Wordlessly, she nodded. If she opened her mouth she was afraid of what would come out. Or wouldn't.

"See you then," he said.

Fearscape by Nenia Campbell

Chapter Eleven

Getting dressed that morning was an exercise in futility. What did one wear gearing up for such a confrontation? And how did one don armor for a weakness of the heart? Normally, Val went to her mother for fashion advice but in this case she knew what the answer would be. *Don't confront him. Run.*

It was good advice. Sensible. Val disregarded it.

She settled on a white camisole, a green button-down henley, and a pair of mid-length khaki shorts that made her butt look big. Lisa would not have approved of the outfit at all, shorts aside. She would have pointed out that Val looked like she should be going door-to-door, peddling copies of *The Watchtower*. Val put her hair into pigtails for good measure.

Her mother blinked when she saw her. "Is that what you're wearing?"

"Yup."

Mrs. Kimble seemed about to say something. Then she closed her mouth and shook her head. "Are you ready to leave?"

As ready as I'll ever be. Val nodded.

"I have a doctor's appointment, so you'll have to take the

bus home today. Do you need money for the fare?"

"No."

"All right then." Her mother dropped her off at the front gates. "Have a good day."

Val walked to her classroom, unable to shake the feeling that the other students were laughing at her. She sat in the corner of the art room, sandwiched between two girls she didn't know who kept shooting her dirty looks. Val tried not to notice and spent the next half hour pretending nothing existed beyond the bowl of fruit Ms. Wilcox had placed up front for that day's lesson.

As she sketched, she studied Gavin from the corner of her eye. He made no attempts to talk to her, which she took as a good sign. He did smile at her, though. It chilled her, that his smile could make his face look so handsome and yet still be so cruel. And then she wondered if she had imagined the cruelty, because she had never really fixated on it before.

You're supposed to be drawing.

It was just that Gavin was so fascinating. Val had never met a boy like him before: he was so mature, so intense and mysterious — oh, and brilliant. Even sexy, she admitted to herself. But what did she really know about him as a person? She had spent more time with him than she had with Lisa these past few weeks, and yet she knew him about as well as Emily Abernathy.

No. Less. Something that did not bode well.

Don't think about that. Draw.

Her fruit kept coming out lopsided. She couldn't keep her hand steady. The eraser on her pencil had been worn clear down to the metal cap.

James kept shooting her these incredulous little glances. What James knew about fashion could fill a thimble and leave plenty of room for one's finger besides, and Val began to worry that she'd overdone it. If James had noticed then Gavin almost certainly had, and unlike James, he would know why.

Val glared at her drawing of the fruit. *Stupid James.*

She sighed.

No. Stupid Val.

School drudged on, slowly as a day in purgatory.

English was no better. Val's essay on *Titus Andronicus*, which she had done in place of the film, was returned to her by Mrs. Vasquez with a grim-looking "C" at the top. Her reading quiz for *Wuthering Heights*, which they had started just last week, earned her an equally dismal 6/10.

Preoccupation with the stalker and Gavin's intense and unequivocal attention had diminished her ability to focus on schoolwork. Val had mixed up quotations from Nelly Dean and Zillah, and had written a hackneyed, self-referential response to the question regarding whether or not Heathcliff was "evil" or a "victim of evil."

Val's argument had been, simply, that Heathcliff had not always been evil, but he had been *bad*, and 'bad' had progressed to 'worse' as he was gradually corrupted by the morally stunting environment of the manor, which eventually culminated into a pretty good approximation of evil.

The teacher had written, *Next time provide more concrete examples and include quotations from the text.*

If only she had taken the quiz this week instead of last. She certainly had more concrete examples of evil under her belt now. She only half-listened as Mrs. Vasquez used *Wuthering Heights* to segue into *Romeo and Juliet.* She lectured about star-crossed love and screwed-up characters so ill-suited to one another that they repelled even as they attracted, thus dooming their stories to certain tragedy. All Val could think about was 5 o' clock, and whether or not she was dooming *herself* to certain tragedy. The closer she got to 5 o' clock, the more she began to suspect that she was. This was a bad idea.

Even the video on pregnancy in Health (which prompted all the boys to make retching noises and all the girls to cross their legs beneath their short skirts and declare that they would never, under any circumstance, subject themselves to such a painful and humiliating procedure and that's exactly what adoption was for, thank you very much) couldn't rouse Val from her thoughts, even long enough to be nauseated.

I'm an idiot. I should cancel.

But she didn't have his phone number — he had never offered it, and she hadn't asked.

Why didn't he give it to me?

Maybe his plan sucked. Maybe he had one of those Go-Phones. When they had talked about his family he'd implied that he paid for everything himself, out of pocket. But still.

If I meant something to him, he'd want me to be able to contact him. I mean, even James's number is in my cell phone.

The bus dropped off Val a block from her house and she

fretted the whole walk home. As she walked through the door she caught a glimpse of herself in the foyer mirror and winced, wondering if she should change into something a little less ridiculous. But then he'd know that she had changed for him, which was precisely what she had been trying to avoid in the first place. Her reflection's face fell.

I really do look like a dork. No wonder people laughed at me.

She poured herself a glass of water she didn't drink and ended up spending the next hour and fifteen minutes pacing. At five o' clock sharp the white Camaro pulled up in front of Val's house. She wrote her mother a note on the fridge, grabbed her bag, and latched the front door behind her.

Gavin reached over to unlock the door for her. He was wearing a fitted leather jacket, which he definitely hadn't been wearing earlier, and she realized with an unexpected lurch that his arms were just as muscular as they had been in his archery photo on the school's website.

"Good afternoon," he said. And was it her imagination or was there an edge of anticipation in his voice?

"Hi."

"I like your outfit."

"Are you making fun of me?"

His lips quirked. "Perhaps a little. No track uniform today?"

She gulped. "No."

"How disappointing." He flipped the blinker on. "I'm surprised your mother let you come out to play with me."

"What?"

"She didn't seem to care for me." His eyes met hers briefly as he turned to signal over his shoulder.

"I didn't tell her," Val said, surprising herself with her boldness. He didn't have to know about the note she'd left taped on the fridge. "She doesn't know."

"Naughty girl." And he smiled to himself, as if he found that thought, and the images which accompanied it, particularly pleasing, in a way that made Val feel slightly less foolish about the knife with the broken handle secreted away in the pocket of her shorts.

Just in case, she'd told herself, feeling as if she were mad.

As before, he parked inside his garage though it wasn't raining. "There have been some problems with vandals in the area," he explained, though she hadn't asked. "They cruise around the neighborhood stealing things — petty theft."

"I don't think they'd steal your car."

The moment she said the words she realized how that sounded, but instead of looking offended he laughed. "Not for the car alone, perhaps, but I keep some valuable things in there."

"Like what?" *Like a body?*

He gave her a measured look. "I'm a dealer."

"Of *drugs?*" Val blurted.

"Of antiques." He located the house key and fitted it in the lock. "I buy, sell, and trade." He pushed open the door and waited.

She squeezed by, thinking over what he'd said. That fit in with his possessive, acquisitive nature. It was logical that he'd want to own things, as well as people. He probably considered them on the same scale. *If he even is the stalker*, she reminded herself sternly albeit without much gumption. *You don't have proof yet.* Distantly, she heard herself say, "You're kind of young."

Gavin shrugged. "It causes clients to underestimate me."

I won't be making that mistake, she thought.

"Can I get you something to drink? Coffee? Tea? Water?"

The way her stomach was jumping around, putting anything into it, even liquid, seemed like a bad idea. Val started to refuse and then realized that his waiting on her would buy some extra time to think. "Coffee, please."

"How do you take it?"

"Um — no milk. Some sugar."

"All right. Go ahead and sit down." He gestured expansively. "Make yourself comfortable. I won't be long."

Take your time. "No rush," she said, trying to smile. He left, and it was as if a weight had been lifted from her lungs. She sat down at the chessboard. The pieces were set up from another game. Black had more pieces but White had the king backed into a corner — something even Val, with her minimal experience on the board, knew wasn't good.

She couldn't recall much from the previous lesson. Most of what she'd learned had flown right out of her brain when he'd kissed her. Oh, god, that kiss — she'd barely remembered her own name. Val quashed that thought, grimacing when she felt her cheeks glow. She knew how the pieces moved. Vaguely. She remembered what castling was. Vaguely.

She knew how to kiss. Vaguely. But, as with chess, Gavin was vastly more experienced in that field, as well. Who had he been kissing? If the other girls in school shared Lisa's views of him, he would be hard-pressed to find one willing to date him. *Or maybe not.* He'd changed her mind swiftly enough.

Chess. You're supposed to be thinking about chess.

The pieces on the board slowly came back into focus as her thoughts cleared a little. She thought she might be able to remember the fundamentals of the game once she got into the swing of things, but that wasn't the difficult part of chess. The difficult part of chess was anticipating your opponent's moves and building a suitable defense and offense tailored to each individual's specific style of play.

Val glanced at the stairs. *Both on and off the chessboard.*

A sound from the kitchen made her focus guiltily on the aforementioned. On the edge of the table was a leather journal. The cover was scuffed and faded and looked quite old. One of his antiques? She opened it up, after darting a quick look at the kitchen, revealing yellowed pages. Queues of numbers and letters formed large columns that marched on for entire pages. She flipped through them, frowning. Was it some kind of code? If so, there was no key.

"It's chess notation, Valerian. Hardly confidential."

Val jumped and the book fell to the floor with a thud that made her start all over. It was as if he'd read her mind. "I wasn't — "

"Spying?" He set their coffee on the table and bent to pick up his journal. Her reaction had appeared to entertain him, if his smile was anything to go by. "I see. Very subtle."

She folded her arms and tried to look composed. "You write down your games?"

"I do, yes, but this isn't mine; it's my father's. I was studying a few of his winning games. He was a chess player," he added, casually.

"He was?" *Was he a stalker, too?*

Gavin set the journal aside. "Mm. A very good one, too, though I think I may be better than he was now. I'm a bit out of practice."

"Really," said Val. "What was his name?"

"Something Spanish. He was from Spain. The resemblance is supposed to be quite close, though I've only the word of others on that." He leaned his head on his hand, watching her sip her coffee. Almost as an afterthought, he added, "Of course, chess wasn't the only skill he had mastered — if my mother is to be believed."

Val choked on her coffee.

"But then again, one cannot rely entirely on stereotypes to shape one's world view. Even if they are generally true. Experience is everything. Don't you agree, Val?"

She couldn't look at him. "I don't know."

"Hmm. No, I suppose you wouldn't. Well," his tone lost some of its edge. "Do you prefer White or Black?"

"Excuse me?"

"Which color would you like to play?"

"Oh. Um. Black."

"Interesting choice." He rotated the board so that her chosen color was on her side. Since he made no move to do so himself, Val restored the pieces to their proper places. She couldn't shake the feeling that he was testing her, though what the test was, and what the implications were, she had no idea. He offered no comment when she finished so she assumed she had passed.

For now.

Fearscape by Nenia Campbell

She wished he would stop looking at her like that, though.

"Your move," he said softly.

He'd moved one of his pawns. The one in front of his queen. *Right. White goes first.*

"You are jumpy, aren't you?" he said, as she moved the pawn in front of her rook with a shaking hand. "Always so edgy. Perhaps I shouldn't have given you that coffee."

"No — I'm just nervous."

He moved his bishop. "Are you planning something treacherous, Valerian?"

Val nearly choked again. "Why do you say that?"

"I get the feeling you're looking for something." He toyed with the chain around his neck and looking at it made Val want to blush. "Something that should concern me."

She bit her lip and did not respond as she moved another pawn. As if he expected this move he immediately brought out his knight. Val retaliated passively by moving another pawn, avoiding the one he'd set out before. With a slight shake of his head, Gavin moved the knight again and she stared at the board, trying to figure out what he was doing. He rarely moved the same piece twice in a row unless he was rallying an attack.

Is he after my king?

Of course he was. That was the entire point of the game. Stupid question.

Val glanced at his face. He arched an eyebrow. "Yes?"

"Nothing," she muttered.

Somewhere within the recesses of the house, a grandfather clock chimed the hour.

"You know, you never answered my question."

She looked up from the board again. "What question?"

"Are you planning something?"

"No!" she said, her voice too high.

"Not even on the board, Val?" His lips parted into a smile. "You're blushing, by the way."

Val clapped a hand to her face. It felt hot. Grudgingly, she moved the pawn in front of her king up two squares, giving her king room to escape if he had to. No way would she allow him to get pinned, the way he had in the last game that had ended so gruesomely.

She really did wish he would stop looking at her. That

cool amusement stabbed at her heart with a dozen icy knives each time their eyes met across the table. Once or twice she found herself staring at his shirt which, in his casual slouch, was pulled taut over his lean chest.

Both his attire and his careless posture seemed scandalous when paired with what he had insinuated earlier about his father. Had Val pursued that line of thought further, she might have suspected that he was trying to seduce her — but she was too focused on getting upstairs.

"Careful," he said, when she reached for another pawn.

"What? Why?"

He didn't elaborate.

And then she saw the danger. She started to move her rook to castle, but Gavin caught her by the wrist. "I'm afraid you can't do that. I have you in check," he drew her attention to the king, "And you can't castle out of check. Ever."

She couldn't believe he'd trapped her so quickly.

He released her, smiling contentedly. "It's called a fork. There's no way out, so you may as well decide which piece you would hate least to lose."

She stared at his knight with a feeling of panic, her skin

still tingling where he'd brushed her as if his touch had left a brand. She moved her queen to take his knight and he captured the offending piece with his bishop, setting the black queen on his side of the table.

"That was a very bad move, my dear. The worst, actually. You should have let me take the rook."

"I didn't want you to take any of them."

Gavin laughed. "You can't protect all the pieces. That is not how the game is played."

"I can try."

"My, my. Such an idealist. You need to learn how to be more cold-blooded if you are to beat me at this game."

Val moved another pawn. "How?"

"By being prepared to sacrifice everything, at any cost, in order to win."

It's been long enough, I think. I've drunk more than enough coffee to make my break without being suspicious.

"That sounds pretty heartless."

"It's a heartless game."

So they agreed on something.

"Running away from me again, Val?" Val's heart stopped.

For one horrible, irrational moment, she thought he'd used his chess master intellect to read her with the same uncanny accuracy he used on the chessboard. But no, he was talking about the game, always the game, moving his pawn closer towards the one she had just moved.

"Of course I am," she said. "You just took my queen."

"Ah, yes. Well. Just remember," he told her. "If you run from me, I will pursue."

The game went on, her taking some of his pieces, him taking even more of hers. There was no question who would win; it was only a matter of when. Gavin had, in a brief amount of time, captured both knights, a bishop, and a rook. Val watched the board with slightly glazed eyes, watching her pieces being taken from her one at a time, and then sat up abruptly.

His queen was open, and her remaining bishop was in the perfect position to take it.

Was it a trap? His face, when she looked at him, revealed nothing. The perfect poker face; he'd probably beat her at that game, too. It had to be a trap. He was far too good to make such a mistake. And yet, she wondered. Because everyone, even a master, could make foolish errors ….

Then she saw it.

A pawn, a simple pawn, which he had sneaked over to her side of the board several turns ago. She hadn't paid it much mind at the time since she was so busy thwarting attacks made by more principal pieces, and it had steadily been advancing this entire time. If she took his queen, the pawn would promote and she would lose the game. If she took his pawn, he would take her bishop, and she would lose the game.

She was damned if she did, damned if she didn't. In either case, it was checkmate in one.

That was when it clicked for her, staring at the glaring case of catch-22 that the board had morphed into. Her stalker was fond of such systematic annihilation, as well, pursuing her with an avidity that bordered on sadistic.

Val tugged at the hem of her shirt. "Where's your bathroom?"

That made him laugh again. A lighter laugh than before, less menacing, which made her wonder if she had imagined the sinister natures she'd attributed to him. But she knew she hadn't, and she wasn't sure which scared her more: his mercurial temperament, or his ability to hide it.

"Middle door," he said, folding his arms behind his head. "Second floor. Don't be long."

(If you run from me, I will pursue.)

The upstairs rooms were just as Spartan in décor as the ones downstairs. Despite the house's relative size, he didn't seem to go in for personal effects. Behind the first door was a closet, empty except for some winter coats and a handful of cleaning supplies.

The next door was the promised bathroom, which was spotlessly — almost obsessively — clean. She closed the door with a loud slam sure to carry down the stairs.

Behind the third door was a study. It must have been a bedroom, originally, because the door off to the side linked to the room next door, which actually was a bedroom. Twin bedrooms.

Val looked around. An antique desk took up half of one entire wall, crafted from aromatic wood that brought to mind a medieval forest. The chair placed in front of it was anachronistically modern. On the shelves of the desk were old books, some of which she recognized from class (including that hateful play, *Titus Andronicus*), others a mystery.

Against the far wall was a glass case filled with real butterflies, all of them long dead. Val's heart faltered as she stared at the limp, jewel-toned bodies with the silver pins neatly skewering their thoraxes, and her hands pressed against her own belly in unconscious sympathy.

Slips of paper beneath each specimen identified the genus in an elegant hand. *Cupido minimus* was the verdigris butterfly that seemed crafted from eyelet lace. *Boloria selene* had wings as bright and lovely as stained glass windows. *Apatura iris* was a large, beautiful butterfly with star-spangled indigo wings. There were many others, and Val now saw that the case bore an additional label at the bottom, in the same hand: *Butterflies of Europe.*

The penmanship was similar to the one she'd glimpsed in the chess journal, the capital Bs and As bearing the same sharp, hooked slashes through their middles. Was this collection also inherited from Gavin's father, then? What a cruel man he must have been to kill such helpless, innocent creatures. She ran her finger down the frame and then turned away, unable to look at them any longer.

Turning had brought her around to face the desk once more. The case of butterflies had settled things, in a way, giving her enough conviction to override her guilt. She sat in the leather chair and began to go through his drawers. There were a lot of office supplies, art supplies, and bundles of papers that looked like financial statements.

What did you expect? A written testimony of his guilt? No, not exactly, but something more helpful than — she glanced down at the paper — stupid tax returns. She scooted forward to replace the papers and lost her balance, her knee coming into sharp contact with the drawer. The pain was immediate and brought tears to her eyes, and she reached out to still the clatter.

Wait — why was it rattling like that? There was nothing in there to make such a sound.

She peered into the drawer again, pulling aside the papers. As she did so, the bottom of the drawer lifted a few centimeters. *A false bottom. His drawer has a false bottom.* Val glanced over her shoulder, and then lifted out the wooden tray, holding her breath.

A journal. He was hiding a journal, similar to the one downstairs, but newer and less scuffed, and beneath it, a sketchbook she had never seen him bring to class before. She said the sketchbook aside, blinking in shock when she read the words *"I saw two lions mating today,"* written in a hand similar to, but more elegant than, the writing on the case of butterflies.

This wasn't a chess log, then. This was an actual journal. His.

Val glanced at the door again, then smoothed out the pages and began to read.

Fearscape by Nenia Campbell

Chapter Twelve

I saw two lions mating today.

Not in real life, but in Biology. The teacher showed us another video. Since he is losing his job at the end of this year, I suppose he doesn't see the point. Of anything. I've seen him drinking in his car before class, and from a hip flask, no less. I think he knows that I know. How else to explain that I never turn anything in and yet am still able to maintain a cozy A in the class?

But anyway, the lions.

We're learning about sexual education, the underlying assumption being that the students of this school are not conducting their own independent studies of the subject on a nightly basis. Though this does not explain why the textbook chapter reads more like a waiver than an instructional guide.

Regardless, human mating cannot be shown in class so animal mating must suffice. Horses. Apes. Dogs. We had to suffer through an entire menagerie. But then came the lions and I could tell right away that this pair was going to be different.

The female was growling, hackles raised, as they circled each other. The male pounced, forcing the female down to the ground with his powerful forelegs. She tried to fight him. With a growl, the male sank his teeth into her throat, increasing the pressure until she lowered her head to her paws in submission. Then he mounted her and took his worthy prize at his leisure.

In the dusty sunlight of the African savanna the two of them looked like burnished idols.

What would it be like, I wonder, to have such power over a woman? To feel her beneath you, as beautiful and golden and lovely as the sun, half-willing, half-resistant? To know that you have her by the throat? I should like to have such an experience for myself.

But I want someone untamed — who, like a wild foal, I can break and reshape the way I wish. There is a kind of sweetness required for proper submission combined with a latent sensuality. Such women are innocent but only because they need someone to provide them with the release they would be otherwise incapable of seeking out on their own.

I have been studying a freshman girl in my art class who seems promising. She does track and field. I saw her while sitting in the bleachers one day, completing a rough sketch for Art — I can't even remember what the subject was, so transfixed was I by the way she ran.

She looked so wild and free out there in the field. It took me a moment to place her as the demure girl with the strange name who never breathes a word. The uniform, too, revealed a body of which I had never before had cause to take notice. But I'm paying attention now.

Whoever she is, I want her.

And I've been drawing her, though she doesn't know it. I drew us, together, cloaked in the darkness of the Biology classroom — me as the lion, her as the lioness, her head turned to the side to bare her throat to me. I clothed her in the skins of her prey, the claws and teeth and bones of her various kills strung on a necklace that hung heavily at her breast.

Myself, I drew in fur. Black, instead of gold, to better hunt among the shadows. Blood smeared on my hands and chest, my hand around her neck, the other tangled in her hair. And all the while, my pants grew tighter until I could scarcely breathe and I had to leave the classroom.

She raises feelings in me so powerful that there are times I don't know what I'll do. I think I might hurt her if I get too close. No. I know I will. Because the thought of hunting her instills in me the same thrill as the men who chase a vixen through the wood. And then I consider my plans for the future, and how a woman such as this could destroy them should I happen to be caught.

But then, what if she wants to be hurt? What if, like a flint to tinder, I can coax her to flame? To burn for me, and only me? And I remember that girl running against the wind, and I know that there's no going back. I am her future — and she is simply that: mine.

■□■□■□■

Her name is Valerian. It suits her, but then again, I expected no less.

Some cultures believe that knowing someone's name — their true name — gives one power over that individual's soul. I am not given to superstition, but it is an interesting sentiment. Knowing her name certainly gives me access to more information to a strikingly apropos effect.

I like seeing how close I can get before she is aware of my presence. There are times when her eyes seem to lock with mine, and there are times when she is painfully oblivious. Today, for example, I could have reached out and grabbed her. I could have stayed silent and watched her.

But I am a gentleman at heart, and so I left her a gift. A red rose, for passion. I was tempted to leave her a sprig of fresh jasmine, as well, but that seemed tastelessly forward. Perhaps for the best, considering the rejection with which my offering was met.

Interestingly, she chose to keep the poem. Sentiment — or caution? I suspect the latter but it amuses me to think of her as a romantic, so easily seduced by pretty words and empty promises.

My observations have accorded me with far more than I anticipated. I must admit that I am very pleased by what I have seen so far. Very pleased.

That friend of hers is cause for some concern. She sees right through me — or thinks she does. In any case, she sees enough to know not to like it. Clever girl. She, too, is lovely, but cold and hard — and far too conniving. Hardly worthy of my time and attention at all, though her feisty repartee was quite entertaining. Hate list, indeed.

When the two of them left I studied the kittens trying to see what Val saw in them that held her so. Is it the innocence and helplessness that she finds so appealing? The thought makes me smile, for that is exactly what it is about her that keeps me in her thrall.

The kitten bared its fangs at me when I picked it up for

examination. I held its chin aloft so it could not bite or move its head, staring directly into its wide blue eyes as I waited for it to cease spitting and struggling. Eventually it lost interest in biting me and when its small body stilled, I relaxed my hold. Tentatively, it sniffed my fingers and, eyes slightly lowered, rubbed its cheek against the knuckles of my hand. I stroked it obligingly, though absently.

She is good with animals. I've seen that. She can coax the stray tabbies from the brush, to take food from her hand and even, on occasion, to let her stroke their fur. They do not fear her, the way they do me, and yet in her own roughshod way she does project a vague air of competence that is both unselfconscious and formidable. A protector. I suspect that it is this the animals are responding to, that makes them trust her so implicitly.

A sudden tickling sensation brought me back to the present. The kitten was getting restless, and had begun to squirm in an attempt to pour itself over the side of my hand. The claws that had cut Val were retracted but that would soon change. The little creature was getting impatient. I gave it a final pat before setting it down with the others.

There is a freshness to her that does, indeed, remind me of flowers — Val, I mean. Not the kitten. *And her skin must be so soft, so delicate, to be wounded so easily. My fingers can wrap around her wrist and still touch.* The bones of her wrist were so fragile, and nestled between them her pulse thrummed hummingbird fast.

Because of me? I wonder.

■□■□■□■

I submitted the order for my cap and gown. I can't believe I have less than three months left in this tedious place. I'm considering applying to a program for Animal Behavioral Science, or perhaps even Psychology. It amuses me how everyone is under the misguided impression that their thoughts and emotions are opaque, when their bodies lay everything bare all the while.

I look forward to disillusioning them.

That boy, for example. He so clearly wanted to impress her, to make her feel poorly about herself. Poorly enough to settle for second best if he gets shot down by the other girl he's been sniffing around, far less pretty but a good deal more willing.

I almost laughed when his plan backfired, and he found himself cast as the one spurned. And I watched his eyes flick to her continually throughout the entire class. As if he was wondering whether he might have made a foolish choice and found the answer *rather poor.*

Yes, she does look very enticing in green, doesn't she? I think so, too. It gives her eyes a distinctly feline glow and brings out the lush, red ripeness of her lips. She has a gorgeous mouth. When I think of all the possibilities of what I could have her do with it, I feel faint.

As I imagine you did, when you watched her. And repented.

But she won't have to settle for you, anymore, will she? Not anymore.

I saw the way you looked at me. Locking eyes is considered aggressive in the animal kingdom. It makes me wonder if perhaps you want to go head to head with me. Over a female, no less. Very appropriate, but not at all wise. In fact, I really don't think you want to fuck with me at all. You're welcome to try, though. The human species would do well to be rid of your genes.

Oh, Val, what are you doing to me? It's been a long time since I've felt so alive. So ready. So eager. I would do anything to keep this feeling bottled up inside. Anything.

■□■□■□■

I feel I could kill. I feel that I might like it. And I know that this should scare me, but it doesn't. It excites me. I am in Plato's cave, watching the shadows and fraught with the desire to hunt what casts them. I close my eyes and at night I dream of blood.

■□■□■□■

You suspect, don't you? You're not sure what — not yet — but you suspect. I doubt you'd be able to guess, though you always do seem able to surprise me. You have no idea how close I was to taking you up on that innocent little gaffe of yours. How much it taxes me to play the role of the cavalier gentleman. Not that I mind. I admit, it's diverting. I've always had a penchant for theater. I suppose that makes you my ingénue.

But I suspect there's a bit of the femme fatale in you, as well. Why else would you pursue your own pursuer, if not to satisfy your own baser instincts? I've seen the way you look at me, when you think I'm not watching. That wasn't an innocent glance. You were undressing me with those bewitching green eyes of yours.

I wonder, would you let me kiss you now? Caress you? Would you let me tie you up? You've already let me touch you. How far would you let me go, I wonder, before it became too far?

■□■□■□■

I grow weary of utilizing the same subjects, over and over. Not even Val can satisfy me — not on canvas alone, at any rate. Ms.

Wilcox suggested I try my hand at abstract art. I nearly laughed; "abstract art" is an affected contradiction, an oxymoron.

But I could not say that. I have a role to play for Ms. Wilcox, too. And so I lauded her for her wisdom, even as I made note to disregard it.

Perhaps a chess game, at a critical turning point. It has been a while since I thought of chess. Shaping a game out of nothingness — I could do that, I think. I keep my old chess logs in a drawer. I can amalgamate the best games, to create a striking work of brilliancy —

But with a twist. Blood seeping from a felled piece, perhaps. I must think on this.

■□■□■□■

I have been denying myself the privilege of watching her run, savoring the anticipation and letting it culminate, and then breathe, like a fine wine. I admit, I was afraid that the effect of seeing her would gradually diminish with repeat exposure, but my fears appear ill-founded. All the same; it is not an experience to be squandered away.

Recent events, however, have made me feel entitled to a bit of stolen pleasure. I received a letter today from Her, asking me when I planned to visit. I was most displeased, as I thought I had made it quite clear that I had no intention of returning to New Jersey.

However, Anna-Maria is getting married and this event appears to require my attendance. She is my least favorite of my sisters. There is too much of our bitch mother in her. Any man foolish enough to open himself to her claws is well deserving of his fate. I may have to go.

I watched her — Val, not my sister — from the shadows beneath the bleachers. Empty cups and cartons and stubbed-out cigarettes littered the ground at my feet. There was something exquisite about the darkness, the rot, when juxtaposed against Val running through the rain. Something real. It was true, what I'd told her before, about disliking posing.

She acts differently around me. Tentative, skittish — almost fearful. It's very amusing and not at all like the woman I have come to know from the track field: fierce, determined, confident. Despite her mild temperament, this hidden side to her leads me to suspect that she will be a ferocious lover when I manage to get her into my bed.

I can easily imagine her nails digging into my shoulders, the bite of her teeth in my lip, her breathy screams —

I unbuckled my belt.

This is why I watch from the shadows. Not out of shame, but so I can watch, observe, and do as I please. Unseen. Unheard. But very much a part of the background. I would be lying if I said that the prospect of caught didn't amuse me a little. Among other things.

Oh, Val.

■□■□■□■

I had her in my net for a few precious moments. She was very ambivalent towards imprisonment, which did not surprise me. However her continued wariness towards me in spite of my efforts did. She is more perceptive than I gave her credit for, and I cannot but respect her all the more for it. She trembles just like a butterfly when she is in my arms.

■□■□■□■

She slammed the covers closed. There was more, but she was unwilling to go on. She'd had enough. More than enough. She looked at the sketchbook with dread. Her hands were sweating. She wiped them on her shorts, causing the fabric to darken, and flipped through the pages.

A wave of dizziness crashed over her as she recognized her own face staring out at her. *Oh god.* She dropped the sketchbook back in the drawer and replaced the bottom. She couldn't remember how to breathe. Those drawings were not the imaginings of a sane man.

"Val?"

It was like something out of a horror movie, hearing his voice echo through the hall. She heard a knocking sound, just a few doors down, and covered her mouth to stifle a scream when the bathroom door opened and then slammed shut just as quickly. His footsteps were moving down the hallway with purposeful precision.

He knows.

Val pinched the journal beneath her arm and headed for the door to the adjoining bedroom. She closed it quietly behind her, struggling to keep in the loud sob threatening to bubble straight past her lips. It was an irrational thought, for an irrational situation.

Reality, for Val, had swiftly become a nightmare.

As the office door opened a horrible thought occurred to her. *Did I close the drawer?* She honestly couldn't remember — reading the journal, and its contents, had wiped her mind so clean as to render it a blank slate. Papers rustled. Val's nausea grew. She hadn't heard him open the drawer. *Oh, god, then he knows. He knows I know.*

And he would kill her to keep his secret. No. Not kill her. Not right away, at least. Images from the sketchbook flooded her head. *Worse.*

"I know you're nearby, Val."

She stared at his bedroom closet.

"You have something of mine."

He was toying her, like a cat with a mouse. Enjoying her terror, basking in it. Well, she wasn't going to wait around for him to find her in some nightmarish game of hide-and-seek. She bolted for the closet and had only just slid the door closed behind her when the office door burst open.

Something behind her jangled as she nudged her way towards the back. The muffled vacuum of the closet amplified the sound into a startling gong. She reached out automatically to still it, and inhaled sharply when she realized what it was she was holding. Handcuffs. Metal handcuffs.

Her back hit the wall and one of the coats fell on her, smothering her with the sandalwood scent of whichever aftershave or wash he was so fond. Beneath the coat she quivered, hugging the journal to her chest. *He's completely insane.*

The closet door opened. Clothes were shoved aside and light flashed on the other side of the coat as the contents of the closet were bared to unseen eyes. Val didn't breathe. She wanted to check, to ensure her entire body was covered, but to move would mean death.

Please, please, please —

She screamed when she felt herself being lifted into the air, coat and all, and then again, with a renewed sense of fear when he yanked the coat off her head and she realized where she was. "You seem to have lost your way," he said mildly, though there was nothing mild about the expression on his face.

She backed away and jumped when her back brushed against the wooden headboard. Gavin watched her for a long, terrible moment and then picked up the journal which had fallen from her numb fingers. He thumbed through the pages, an odd smile on his face, before tossing the book aside. It hit the floor with a hollow thud that made her jump again.

"Or perhaps not," he said, inclining his head in her direction, "perhaps you were looking for something —

something specific."

"I don't — "

"Let's not play games, Val. We both know that you read the journal — but you never stopped to consider the fact that I might want you to find it."

She stiffened. "I didn't read it."

"Then why are you so afraid? I've given no sign of wanting to harm you. In fact, I've taken great pains to produce the exact opposite impression."

It took her a moment to speak. "Please don't hurt me."

"Don't look at me like that. It won't help your situation."

"I won't tell anyone. Just let me go, and I'll never tell a soul."

"You have such soft lips, you know — and a beautiful mouth. Your first kiss was very pleasurable indeed, though that kiss in my living room was a vast improvement. If you manage to do better still, I'll let you go right now."

"That's all?"

She wanted to believe, but didn't in the slightest. It sounded too good to be true and experience had taught her that this was most likely the case.

"What if I refuse?"

"You wouldn't like it," he said.

Val thought of the handcuffs in his closet and believed him.

Chapter Thirteen

Such a simple thing, a kiss.

Yet in the state of hypersensitivity brought on by fear, in which she was as painfully aware of her body and its surroundings as a creature comprised solely of raw skin and nerve endings, a kiss seemed like a very large price to pay.

Extortionate.

Would a man, even an obsessed man, go to such lengths for a mere kiss? Even Val in all her childlike naivete couldn't bring herself to believe this, however much she wanted to.

"Well?"

Her breathing sounded too loud. She had never been more aware of her own fragile mortality. *You've kissed him before*, she reminded herself. *Lots of times. He's not any different.*

But she was. And now she knew his most intimate thoughts and had found, to her horror, that her romantic idealization of him as the tragically misunderstood artist was just that: an ideal, now shattered, with reality gleaming through like sharp slices of mirror reflecting light. He was ruthless, cold, and he wanted her to be like one of the lifeless butterflies in the collection behind his glass cabinet.

Fearscape by Nenia Campbell

An inanimate plaything.

A possession.

A prisoner.

"I'm waiting," he said, regarding her through half-shut eyes.

She had come into the garden expecting summer roses and had instead been caught in a bank of twisted, thorny frost-iced vines.

"Just one kiss?" she confirmed, breathing out a little when he nodded. "And you'll let me go?"

"Quite."

Val's arms shook. She leaned in and pecked him feebly on the mouth. His lips still tasted like coffee. "You're not trying."

And that was when she understood: she was intended to perform the work herself.

An image of a butterfly in a killing jar popped into Val's head, fragile wings straining against the cloyingly sweet miasma coating the delicate membranes with a thin layer of poisonous crystals. Like rime. Or frosted sugar. Not all poison was bitter — some of the deadliest poisons in the world tasted sweet. They were that much more dangerous because of it.

Don't think about that. Turning this situation into a carnival of horrors wasn't going to help. She closed her eyes and covered his mouth with hers. He remained still as a statue, though when she nudged at his closed lips with her tongue he opened his mouth.

She wrote her prayers for salvation in his mouth, with the tip of her tongue, and he made a low sound in the back of his throat that did not necessarily sound like displeasure, though it didn't sound pleased, either. He had yet to reciprocate, and the thought that he might prolong this infinitely until he deemed himself completely satisfied shot into her head.

Evil bastard. She hated him, for the first time. Well and truly hated him. He had her trapped, and he had carefully planned each and every bar of the prison she now found herself in. She channeled that anger, molding herself against him and holding onto his neck to steady herself wishing in her heart of hearts that she was strangling him instead.

His arms wrapped around her waist automatically and his mouth began, at length, to move against hers. Vertigo wrapped around her brain in thick, shimmering mist as he rolled over so that she was on top, dizzied from the fear, the danger, his effects on her body.

Especially his effects on her body.

"That was nice."

"It was?"

"Very." His hands slid onto the shallow indent of her waist with easy familiarity. "But where do you think you're going?" he inquired, as she swung an unsteady leg over the side of the bed.

"You said I could — "

"I don't believe I you permission to leave," he said, and his grip tightened in emphasis. He twisted his hips then, knocking her off-balance. She found herself straddling him. "If you recall, I said your efforts on this occasion had to be superior to the last."

"I kissed you," she said, "Just like you wanted."

"Your technique is flawless but last time you looked considerably more appealing. If I hadn't known I was going to have to give you back …." His eyes darkened and he shook his head. "Suffice it to say that it will be a difficult act to follow."

"You're not going to let me go, are you?" Her voice was hoarse, even to her own ears. "How long to you intend to keep me here? And don't lie to me!" Val knocked his hand away from her when he tried to touch her, blinking back tears. "You're so sick, I don't even want to look at you, let alone *kiss* you — all those things you —" *Drew,* she had been about to say. But then she remembered, he didn't know she'd seen his sketchbook. " — Said," she finished weakly.

"You're welcome to try again. Or try things my way."

A chill filled her. She gritted her teeth, trying to block out the images that rushed at her, in charcoal and watercolor, tinged with passion and violence. "Once more," she choked.

"We'll see," he said mildly.

And that decided it. She leaned in again, and his lips parted in anticipation — and she headbutted him. Hard. He let out a roar, like a wounded bull, but his grip on her waist loosened. She must have surprised him; she had surprised herself. Val scrambled off him and ran, clutching her own throbbing head. She heard him clambering after her.

Something hard jagged into her shoulder. It was the wooden banister. She remembered the knife with the broken handle and produced the little blade just as he was upon her.

"She has claws."

"Stay back."

"I wonder, what else does she have?"

"Stay back," Val repeated, accompanying the command with a jab.

His hand shot out, serpent-quick, to deliver a sharp undercut to her wrist that made her drop the blade in a spasm of pain. She started to bend to retrieve it from the floor but Gavin kicked it aside as he took a step forward, and Val had to veer backwards to avoid his grab for her.

Her weight shifted past her waist, centering in her upper body. She lost her balance. The world spun and she screamed hoarsely as she felt herself falling over the balcony head-first. Somehow, she managed to grab the rails. The carved blocks of wood cut into her sweaty palms but at least it kept her from going over.

Val glanced over her shoulder to get a look at the drop, then let the rest of her body fall over as she jumped the last five feet. She hit the floor with enough force to make her teeth rattle around inside her skull. It occurred to her, as she ran in the direction of the door, that she had no idea where to run — Gavin had driven her over here, and her house was too far to walk.

And I left my purse in his house. With my phone —

Escape. She had to focus on escape. She could deal with the phone later. If she didn't escape, there wouldn't be a later.

She hurled herself against the door with a desperation she hadn't known she possessed. It would not open — and it took a moment for the panicking animal her brain had become to understand that the deadbolt was fastened.

His fingers curled around her wrist as tightly as a handcuff. "I'm not letting you leave."

No, Val thought, with real terror. She cocked back her arm and elbowed him somewhere soft enough to elicit a grunt of pain. He released her. She hooked her foot around his leg and jerked. He fell, though he had the reflexes to throw out his arms to break his fall. She unfastened the deadbolt with fingers that felt as ineffective as rubber as he started to get back up.

Come on. Come on.

It slid free with a loud snap. She twisted the doorknob, hard, and slipped outside. She grabbed the knob on the other side and pulled, trying to shut the front door on him. Behind the oak panel, she heard a chuckle — he was laughing at her, even now, as if her attempts to escape were nothing more than the amusing antics of a child.

She was losing their tug-of-war with the door, so she gave in and rammed her shoulder against it, and her impact, combined with the force of his own momentum, sent him falling back with a thud that shook the windows in their panes.

Val turned and headed for the first house she saw with the porch lights on, and didn't dare look over her shoulder. *Please be home*. She knocked on the door, trying to contain herself because she knew if she looked too crazy nobody would come. *Please, please answer.*

Through the windows, Val could see the bluish flickers of a TV coming from the depths of the house. An older woman came to the door. She was holding a cordless phone in her hand and looked quite cross, though that quickly dissolved as she took in the scene awaiting her.

"Oh my goodness," the woman said, blinking rapidly. "Elinor, I'm going to have to call you back. There's a young girl and — are you all right?" During this entire exchange, the woman kept her hand on the phone, fingers poised over the bottommost digit, ready to use it for a distress call or a weapon, however the situation required.

Wise, Val thought, in a burst of self-pity she hadn't had the time to indulge in. *Wiser than me.*

She opened her mouth to say — what, exactly, she wasn't sure. It didn't matter. Whatever words she thought to utter were immediately drowned in a flood of tears.

That seemed to decide it for the woman and she hesitated only briefly before stepping aside to allow Val entry. The room was lit with soft orange light and spilling with lace trimmings. She led Val into a parlor that smelled strongly of peppermint and mothballs.

A shiver rolled down Val's spine as she watched the woman bolt all three locks.

"Dear?" the woman said, turning around. "What happened? Are you hurt? Did someone attack you?" Her face furrowed, giving her the appearance of a withered peach. "You're not involved in anything criminal, are you? Because if you are, I'll have to mention that when I call the police."

Val made a very small sound that she didn't recognize as

her own.

"What was that? Speak up, dear, my hearing isn't so good. Should I call the police now?"

"Please — " Val wet her cracked lips, chapped from sticky kisses stolen in the dark "I … I want my mom."

Poor thing, the woman thought — and then paused. That really was such a terrible phrase, as if tragedy rendered someone inanimate and helpless, worthy of pity in only the most abstract and impersonal sense. She placed a hand on the girl's trembling back, and she flinched.

"Would you like a peppermint candy?"

Val shook her head, eying the congealed mass of sweets in the glass jar that the woman was proffering. She wanted to vomit. *Oh, god,* she kept thinking, *Oh, god, oh, god, oh, god.*

The woman set the jar back down on the doily-covered table. "When you can," she said, enunciating each word, "You may use the cordless. I'll put it right here."

She set it on the pillow nearest to Val, who stared at it like she'd never seen one before.

"As soon as your mother comes — well, we'll figure that out, then, won't we?" Val did not answer, and the woman nodded decisively to herself. "Good. I think I'll put some tea on. Would you like some tea, dear? It might help."

They don't make tea for what he's done to me.

The woman introduced herself to Val's mother as Beatrice Cooper.

"Here's my number," she said, handing over a yellowed business card, "In case you need me to give testimony or anything like that — though I'm retired now, the number's the same." Mrs. Cooper paused. "Your daughter was running away from someone who clearly wanted to hurt her. It would be my pleasure to put him where people like him belong."

"I can't thank you enough," said Mrs. Kimble. "It was so kind of you — I mean, thank God — "

"I'm just doing my civic duty," Mrs. Cooper said complacently.

Val's mother tried to write her a check but Mrs. Cooper would hear nothing of it.

"Making sure he gets caught will be reward enough."

He won't get caught, thought Val. *I will.*

■□■□■□■

Mrs. Kimble had driven to Ms. Cooper's house with the

intention of threatening her daughter with every punishment under the sun, and then a good deal that weren't. Seeing the teary, trembling ball her daughter had curled into on that woman's couch swiftly changed her mind. She bought Val a Neapolitan milkshake instead. It had been her go-to method when Val was a child, and it was the only thing that came to mind now. Val sipped the drink and sniffled, but said nothing.

Worst-case scenarios flooded through Mrs. Kimble's head. Rather wanting to cry herself, she wrapped Val up in a quilt and installed her on the sofa. Then she dampened a paper towel and began cleaning her daughter's face, her heart breaking when Val flinched at the contact. "Baby," she whispered. "Please. Please tell me what's wrong."

It was as if Val shattered into a thousand words — mute only moments before, she now couldn't stop talking. Even if she wanted to. Especially if she wanted to.

"I'm scared," Val said, once she'd finished.

"We have to call the police."

A swift rush of movement from the sofa. "No!" Val was in her path in an instant, blocking her way to the phone. Her eyes were wide, still wild with terror. "You can't. No police!"

"But Val, honey, we have to — "

"No, we don't!"

"Val, don't be ridiculous. Of course we do. What that boy did to you, he deserves to be locked up. Now get out of the way — "

"No!"

Mrs. Kimble stared at this savage creature her daughter had become. "Val, you can't want to defend him," she said gently, "what he did to you was — "

"I'm not. I'm not defending him. But don't call the police."

Val's mother was torn. "Why on earth not?"

"Because I don't want anyone to know," she whispered.

No, Mrs. Kimble realized, with a sinking feeling in her heart. They would want to put her on the stand, and that horrible boy and his lawyers would tear into her like a pack of wolves, not to mention the news reports, the articles, the gossip. And what if, in spite of her testimony, he went free? All that pain and humiliation would be for nothing.

All at once, she understood.

"No police," she agreed quietly, and Val deflated in her mother's arms. "Why don't you take a nice hot bath? Then change into some pajamas and see if you can get some sleep."

Val nodded, and slunk upstairs.

My poor sweet little baby. Who in their right mind would want to hurt her?

And then Mrs. Kimble realized she had answered her own question.

Fearscape by Nenia Campbell

Chapter Fourteen

Dear Valerian,

Your mother called and e-mailed to let me know you would be missing my class for the rest of the year due to some very tragic personal circumstances. I want you to know I am deeply sorry to hear this; you were one of my favorite students, and I was looking forward to discussing your final project with you (you got an A, in case you wondered).

Please feel free to come by on the last day of school. I'll be cleaning my classroom for the summer. It would be so nice to be able to say goodbye.

Best regards,

Barbara Wilcox

■□■□■□■

To: Valerian Kimble

From: Lisa Jeffries

Subject: OMG

Are you OK? My mom said your mom told her you wouldn't be coming to school for the rest of the year!!! I know that's only a week, but STILL. What happened? Were you in an accident? I'm sorry about making fun of your boyfriend(?)!

Fearscape by Nenia Campbell

I won't do it anymore if YOU JUST TALK TO ME. I miss you. Please tell me if you're okay. Please??

-Lisa

To: Valerian Kimble

From: Lindsay Polanski

Subject: STOLEN PHONE

I think your phone might have been stolen (if you weren't already aware of this)! I was wondering why you hadn't responded to any of my texts so I decided to call you. This guy picked up — definitely NOT you, unless you've gotten a sex change (you haven't, have you? AWKWARD) — and demanded to know who I was and why I was calling.

Naturally, I said, who the hell was asking? This was MY FRIEND'S phone. What was HE doing with it? He hung up on me. I called that asshole back a dozen times and eventually he told me in a very scary voice that I had better stop bothering him or I'd be sorry. After that, I couldn't even get a dial tone. It freaked me out.

P.S. Are you OK? I haven't seen you around campus.

Hope you find the creep with your phone.

 P.P.S. Actually, I take that back. I hope you DON'T find him. He sounds like a total psychopath.

■◘■◘■◘■

To Valerian Kimble:

From: ------

Subject: ------

You gave me quite the chase, didn't you? I'm quite impressed. Also, I must say this: you look even more appealing when you're afraid, so I'll let you run for now.

■◘■◘■◘■

To Valerian Kimble:

From: ------

Subject: ------

Don't flee too far.

■◘■◘■◘■

 Shafts of dusty sunlight speared through the pink curtains, making dust motes flare as brightly as supernovae. The yellow light thawed the temperature of the room and Val began to twist and turn beneath her covers as she began to overheat. When she opened her eyes, beads of sweat dotted her forehead and the bridge of her nose and dampened her hair.

Val gasped, her pupils narrowing to pinpricks as they focused on some unseen terror. She clutched at her chest until the muscles relaxed and her neurons, firing blindly as they scattered like an ant colony attacked by a predator, regrouped, once more allowing for reason.

She collapsed back against her mattress, wincing a little when she came down too hard on a bruise. *I'm here, safe.*

No. Not safe.

She would never be safe again.

She kicked off the sheets with a mutter of disgust, rolled out of bed, and got dressed. Not in her school clothes — the standard jeans and t-shirt — but terry-cloth shorts and a tank top. Val should have been at school enjoying the last day of her freshman year, giggling with friends, signing yearbooks, and saying goodbye to favorite teachers.

Instead, she was bumming around at home, stewing in her own fears. *At least I got to sleep in*, she thought, though when she looked at the clock and saw that it was only 9 AM that proved little consolation — particularly given that her rest had been fractured by intermittent nightmares.

The messages from her friends and teacher were of some comfort. Especially the one from Ms. Wilcox. The rest of Val's teachers were nice enough, but Val was never completely sure whether they actually cared about her, or were just pretending to care because they wanted tenure. Nobody was paying Ms. Wilcox to send Val feel-good messages; it was nice to know somebody cared.

Val wanted to respond but nothing came immediately to mind, and she ended up responding to her friends' messages instead because those were easier. She just reeled off a couple of generic platitudes — you're so sweet, I'm OK, my phone was stolen so I'll call you as soon as I can, thanks for your concern — and hoped that they wouldn't mistake weariness for bitchiness. And then paranoia got the better of her and she ended up deleting all her responses.

I just can't concentrate.

No. More than that, she wanted to be alone.

Supposedly, that was a normal after-effect of trauma. Her mother had said so. The brain got locked in a loop of heightened arousal, and the sympathetic nervous system remained on red alert, sending out the biochemical equivalent of a warning siren. The fear was normal: healthy, even.

So then why do I feel so sick?

Her eyes lit on the final message in her inbox and her mind halted, her index finger frozen over the arrow key.

(I'll let you run for now)

Threat laced through each word with deliberate precision, like pins through a voodoo doll, and fear surged through her veins in a distinctly Pavlovian response.

He hadn't forgiven her for getting away.

He was warning her because he felt certain that it would do her no good, beyond scaring her senseless.

(Don't flee too far)

He believed he would capture her.

She knew she was giving him power over her by analyzing the message in such depth, doing his dirty work. She knew this, and yet she couldn't resist.

She never had been very good at that. Not with him.

A warm, sweet smell wafted into Val's bedroom and her stomach growled.

She padded into the kitchen and stared in surprise at the

image of her mother wearing a flowered apron, bending over their dusty oven as if she thought she was Martha Stewart. "Good morning, Val," she said, in a tone of forced cheer. "I'm making *pain au chocolat*."

Val looked around for a box of pastry mix. There was none. "From scratch?"

"Don't look so shocked," her mother said, "I studied abroad in Paris, you know."

Val hadn't known.

"I got an email from Ms. Wilcox."

"Is that your art teacher? That was kind of her."

"She sounded worried." Her voice caught a little. "What did you tell Principal Hopkins about me?"

"Nothing personal. Just that you were having some family problems. He was very understanding."

Her mother's look was pointed. Val avoided her eyes.

"Thank you," she whispered.

"I still think you should talk to the police — "

"No."

"But if he — "

"*No.*"

Mrs. Kimble stiffened, then nodded. "Okay." She took a tube of dark chocolate from the fridge, letting out her breath as she set it on the counter. "Okay," she repeated. "I just wanted to make sure that you didn't change your mind."

Val folded her arms on the table. "She asked me if I wanted to visit. Do you think I could?"

"What time did she say again? After school? That doesn't sound like a very good idea, Val. I don't want you alone after school hours."

"Please? I miss my friends and teachers. I'm *lonely*."

"I don't want you anywhere even remotely close to that boy, Valerian. He might attack you. He might even kill you."

Val paled. "You think he would? Kill me, I mean?"

"I'd rather not find out," her mother said sharply.

Both of them were silent.

"Does that mean I can never go out again?" asked Val with an edge of bitterness.

"No, honey. Of course not. Look. I'll call your teacher. I'll tell her we're having some safety concerns. About bullying — she doesn't need to know the details, just that you can't be left alone. If we can figure out a way for you to go safely, I'll take you to see your teacher."

Val perked up a little. "When will you call her?"

"As soon as the pastries are done."

Val twitched visibly in her seat while her mother cleaned up the dishes with what seemed, to her, to be deliberate slowness. She fidgeted when her mother pulled the *pain* out of the oven with her ladybug-shaped mitts. Mrs. Kimble had been fixing her with a sideways look the entire time, torn between amusement and aggravation as her daughter's gaze flitted between the clock and the phone. It was nice to see Val still so excited about going outside, though.

There was a bit of a wild streak in Val — she had always loved being out in the sun, hiking, cycling, and especially doing anything related to or involving animals. They had recently signed Val up to work at the shelter as part of her mandatory community service; she had been so excited and wouldn't stop chattering, rather like a little animal herself.

Mrs. Kimble was afraid that what that horrible boy had done would stamp out that bit of life in her daughter, rendering her a pale shadow of her former self. Even now, she looked rather similar to a puppy that has found itself kicked, without warning or reason, and is still looking for the boot.

Mrs. Kimble had read up on some articles about victims of violent assault. Some became agoraphobic and were unable to venture outside without experiencing panic attacks. Others developed post-traumatic stress disorder and experienced vivid and terrifying reenactments of the initial trauma when confronted with stimuli that reminded them of the attack. To Mrs. Kimble's horror, these "stimuli" could be as subtle as an angle of light or shadow, or even just a sound.

According to the information in the articles there could be a delay between the attack and the onset of the symptoms. So maybe it was too early to celebrate. That sick son of a bitch. If her daughter's life was destroyed over this, she resolved, she and her husband would make him pay in full.

For now, she would do her best to get Val through this as painlessly as possible.

"Hi. You've reached Barbara Wilcox. If you're hearing this message, I'm most likely teaching, working in my office, or have already left the campus. You can leave a message, or send me an email at B.R. Wilcox at DHS dot edu. Thank you, and take care."

Mrs. Kimble left a phone message and then went to her office with Val trailing after her and wrote a similar message via email. "There," she said, glancing over her shoulder. "It's sent. Now eat."

"I'm not hungry."

"If you don't eat, you can't leave this house," her mother said. "The choice is yours."

"Maybe I am a little hungry," Val said.

"Good girl. Come on. Let's go eat some *pain*. Chocolate makes everything better."

Not everything, thought Val.

■□■□■□■

Dear Mrs. Kimble,

I'm shocked and upset to hear that Valerian has been the victim of such vicious bullying. She really is such a sweet girl. I honestly can't imagine anyone taking dislike to her, but children can be cruel and irrational.

My classroom is close to the western parking lot, so if you like you can park, wait, and watch to ensure that she enters the building safely. I'll make sure none of the other students stay late.

P.S. Sorry I could not return your phone call! I'm in the middle of teaching a class and the students are under the (mistaken) impression that my using the phone gives them permission to do the same.

Warmest regards,
Barbara

■□■□■□■

"What a lovely woman," Val's mother said, reading the email. "Very charming."

"She's really nice. She always complimented me on my work, even when it sucked."

"Oh, hush," said her mother. "You're a regular Rembrandt."

Val made a face, though it was obvious she was trying hard not to look pleased.

"Why don't you go change?" her mother suggested. "Wear something nice. And maybe we can go out to lunch afterward, when you're done talking with your teacher."

"I'd like that!" said Val, sounding almost like her cheerful self. "It'll be nice to get out of the house, too!"

Val raced upstairs, eager to escape the confines of her

room. It would be nice to get her sketch back, too. She tugged on one of her nice blouses with an ivy motif and a broken-in pair of capris. As she was strapping on her sandals she happened to look at her laptop, still open to the offending message. She slammed her computer shut and walked away with a bounce in her step.

"You look nice," said her mother.

"Thank you," Val replied.

No mention to Gavin's email was made.

The sun was reaching its zenith as they pulled up into the western lot. Val avoided looking at the quad where she and Gavin had often talked in hushed tones beneath the grove of mulberry trees. The last day of school warranted an early dismissal, and the campus was gradually emptying out. Val had never seen her school look quite so sleepy or peaceful before.

"Do you have your phone?" Mrs. Kimble asked.

"Yes, Mom."

"Okay. If you finish early, call for pickup. Otherwise, I'll be here in about an hour."

"Yes, Mom."

"Have fun, Baby," her mother said. "Be safe."

She kept the car's engine running and watched as her daughter made a beeline to the art building. Watched as she tried the handle, found it unlocked, and peered inside the room. Watched as Val gave her a cheery wave and disappeared inside the classroom.

She stayed a few minutes longer, watching, and then slowly she drove away.

■□■□■□■

Mrs. Kimble was sitting down to a cup of tea when the phone rang. Thinking it was Val, she set the mug aside and said, "Hello?"

"Hello," an unfamiliar voice said pleasantly. "May I speak to Mrs. Kimble?"

"This is she."

"Hello! I'm Barbara. Barbara Wilcox. One of Val's teachers — her art teacher."

"Oh, yes. I got your email. Val speaks very highly of you."

"My email?" A pause. "Well, I'm very happy to hear that. Val is a sweet girl, but it's hard to know what's going on behind their foreheads sometimes. Anyway, I've been looking at some of my students' works and Val's was amongst them. The one I'm speaking of is a lovely sketch of a warehouse on the edge of town."

"I know the one you mean. It's an eyesore."

"But Val has brought it to life. Your daughter is very talented, Mrs. Kimble. I wouldn't mind keeping the picture but I wanted to know if either you or Valerian wanted to pick it up. I fear that with many of my students it's a case of out of sight, out of mind. Something they may regret in a few years if they ever need to create a portfolio."

Mrs. Kimble nodded, then remembered the other woman couldn't see it. "That's very considerate of you. I'd be delighted to have the picture — Val rarely shows me her work. You can just send it home with her when you're done."

Another pause. "Excuse me?"

"Well, since she's there with you I thought it might be easier to give her the picture in person. Are they still being graded?"

"No, they're graded," Ms. Wilcox said. "Val got an A. But she isn't here with me."

"Did she leave early? I told that girl — "

"She isn't here at all. I'm in my office. Alone," Ms. Wilcox added, with a touch of irritation.

Fear coursed through Mrs. Kimble's veins like ice water. "But your email said — "

"What email? The one to the students about their final projects?"

Mrs. Kimble went to her computer and recited the email verbatim.

"That's my address," Ms. Wilcox said doubtfully, "But I didn't write that email."

"What?" Mrs. Kimble shrilled. "Then who did?"

"Well ... the only other person who could have possibly sent that email is my student TA, and I'm not sure why he would have done that."

"Your TA has access to your email?"

"Not my password, no, but he was entering grades for me on the computer."

It took Mrs. Kimble a moment to formulate words. "What's your TA's name?"

"Mrs. Kimble, I can't give that information out over the phone — "

"Is it Gavin?" she persisted. "Is your TA named Gavin Mecozzi?"

Ms. Wilcox paused. "How could you — what's going on? Did Gavin do something?"

"Call the police," Mrs. Kimble said. "Drop whatever you're doing and call them right now."

"Mrs. Kimble — "

"And then, if you value your job at all, get to your classroom as fast as you can."

" — what on earth are you — "

"Because if you don't, something terrible is going to happen to my daughter. And I will sue both you and the school for every miserable penny you've got."

" — talking about," the disembodied voice finished. Mrs. Kimble hadn't bothered to hang up. She just grabbed her keys and ran for her car, hoping she wasn't already too late.

The air hung heavy with the smell of paint, wood, and glue. Chemical and organic all at once, it had the same sort of appealing causticity as a drug. Student projects covered the walls and she was delighted to see a few of her own among them.

"Ms. Wilcox?"

Silence prevailed in the empty classroom.

Frowning, Val looked around. A screen saver was running on the glowing monitor. There was a Styrofoam coffee cup in easy reach from the keyboard but when Val picked it up, curiously, it was both empty and cold. She set it back down and looked around, bemused.

Her eyes lit on the glow coming from beneath the heavy wooden door of the storage room. Aha. So she was in the back room then. More pictures were on display in here — older ones, and clearly some of Ms. Wilcox's favorites. Every single artist had talent. There were a number of styles, some done better than others, and she smiled at an Escher-inspired drawing.

The picture she had drawn of the toyger kittens was also on display, now carefully enhanced by water colors. She liked the way it looked, giving the picture a softer edge, though the water had caused the paper to warp a little. But thinking about the kittens reminded her of Gavin.

She slid to the next picture: a chessboard in icy shades of

blue and gray. The pieces, however, were real human beings, and the fallen had collapsed where they'd been taken, staining the marbled tiles with their blood. The only pieces remaining were the black queen and the white king, the two most important pieces in the game.

The perspective was skewed, strange, unnatural — one that would be impossible in real life, and was vaguely reminiscent of the chase scenes in old horror movies. The king carried a bayonet, which added to this image, and towered over the defenseless queen, whose head was lowered in a gesture of defeat, her fair *(red)* hair hiding her expression. The king, however, looked as though he were seconds away from bringing down the weapon in a killing arc.

Oh, she knew who had painted this one. Without a doubt. She'd seen the preliminary version in his sketchbook.

A door slammed behind her and Val stumbled into the metal filing cabinets as she turned around, her eyes widening when she realized who the intruder was. "Look familiar? It's called *Checkmate.* I had to change a few things, but the basic concept remains much the same."

"I don't know what you're talking about," she said

weakly.

He clicked his tongue. "Which picture did you like the best? *Savanna* is my favorite, though for obvious reasons I didn't consider it for submission. I could have made some changes to the content, of course, but that would rather defeat the purpose of the original, don't you think?"

Val couldn't think. She couldn't do anything.

"You put the drawer in backwards," he said. "In case you wondered. But that isn't what I wanted to see you about."

"But Ms. Wilcox — " Val trailed off, connecting the empty room with Gavin's presence. The conclusion was not a pleasant one. "Oh god — where is she?"

"Hmm? Who?"

"What did you do to our teacher? I was supposed to meet her here!"

"Val, Val, Val — what kind of monster do you take me for? I did nothing to her."

"I don't believe you."

"You should. Ms. Wilcox didn't send you that message, you see, though she kindly provided me the means to do so. I did. It was me whom you arranged to meet. Oh, by the way —

I took the liberty of deleting your mother's message. No need for anyone to get hurt. Is there?"

Val flattened herself against the file cabinet. *He's the TA. Ms. Wilcox would have no reason to suspect … to think he would —*

"Now don't get skittish with me." His hands hit the metal on either side of her with twin clangs. "You don't want me to chase you again. Once I catch you, well, I might do anything."

"What does that mean?"

"Use your imagination." His lips brushed hers as he spoke the loose command. Val kept her mouth closed, gritting her teeth so hard they ached. "You do still have one, don't you?" And then his lips were on her throat. She yipped when the sting of his teeth made all the nerves and muscles in her throat bunch up, and she forgot how to swallow.

"I'll scream."

"Be my guest," he said, and the pressure he was putting on her shoulders increased as he began to inexorably drag her down to the ground. Val resisted, but it was like a lone tree trying to stand up to the relentless gales of a hurricane; he would either tear her up by the roots, or snap her in half like a small twig.

"Please …." Something hard slammed against her knees. It was the floor. "Don't do this. *Why* are you doing this?"

"Because it's necessary," he said, gripping her hard by the shoulders, "there is only so much that one can give up freely; I said I wished to possess you in all ways — and I will."

Her head hit the hard floor of the storage room and white sparks burst like fireworks before her eyes.

And then he was on top of her, the solid weight of him keeping her pressed against the cold stone tile. Even though her tears, she could make out his quiet smile of triumph.

"I liked you," her voice broke, "I really liked you. Oh, god, I don't understand — what did I *do*?"

She felt his lips brush against her cheek. For a heartbeat, she felt relief — this was all a mistake, a misunderstanding, her words had struck a chord within him — and then she felt his tongue, tasting the salty tracks of her tears.

"You were too human."

Val twisted her head away so quickly that she hit the stone, and the movement stung. "Lisa was right. You're psychotic."

"Oh, Lisa. The fount of all wisdom. And what other

gospel did she share? Did she tell you I was a big, bad wolf?" He kissed the other side of her throat. "That my big, sharp teeth were all the better to eat you with?"

She opened her mouth to scream, and her breath died as his hand skimmed over her budding breasts through the silk of her blouse. "She was right. I've been hunting you this whole time, waiting for you to stray from the path. But you — you came into the woods after me."

Fearscape by Nenia Campbell

Chapter Fifteen

Fear came in many shapes and forms, and in varying degrees, but until now Val had never experienced the overwhelming terror which resulted from utter helplessness. Seconds ticked by and salvation did not come. And Val came to the grim conclusion that she was completely at his mercy — which was unfortunate, because he didn't seem to have any.

She whimpered when she felt his fingers tease the skin beneath the hem of her shirt. In the confines of her belly, fear formed a hot ball of molten lead.

"Tell me you belong to me."

"No." She squeaked unhappily when his nails raked lightly against her midriff. "No, I won't." She squeezed her eyes shut, putting space between them the only way she knew how. *I don't belong to him.* Then he cupped her breast, as if trying to claw out her heart, and a small, insidious voice added, *yet*. "I won't," she repeated, pathetically, as his lips brushed against her pulse.

"If you say it," his chapped lips scraped her throat with each word, "I might let you go."

How stupid did he think she was, that she would fall for

the same ruse twice? She called him a name, punctuated by several other words she wasn't supposed to know, and a handful of phrases Lisa had used to refer to various ex-boyfriends.

His thumb slipped beneath the cup of her bra and Val froze completely, her speech cut off as neatly as if a switch had been thrown. She was no longer even breathing. Gavin shot her a smile that was distinctly serpentine as he pulled his hand away, running his fingers harmlessly down the center of her ribs. Her heart was hurling itself against her chest as if trying to escape.

Val wished she could do the same.

"You're going to hurt me."

"I can make you feel whatever I want," he went on, in a soft, soothing voice that she didn't believe for one minute.

"You're going to hurt me," she repeated, cracks of fear rifting through her words on each point of impact.

He kissed her, tracing the grooves of her spine as he did with light shivering scratches that made her want to pull away but only caused the body weighing hers down to press against her all the more fully. The words on her lips burned with unspoken promises as he said, "Only a little."

Val's stomach twisted. To her revulsion it wasn't entirely in fear.

Then she saw something that gave her hope. She drew in a deep breath and screamed as loud as she could, gratified when he winced at the shrillness. *I hope I broke his eardrums.* He yanked his hand from her back and clapped it over her mouth hard enough to sting —

And then the door burst open.

Ms. Wilcox had seen many things in her twenty years of teaching, but as she stared, frozen, at the two teenagers tangled up on the floor, she had the passing thought that none of them had ever been quite so bad as this. Val — that sweet, shy girl of whom she was quite fond — was pressed with her back flush against the floor, her arms pinned over her head.

By Gavin. Her TA. Whom she had entrusted with sending emails and making copies and various other privileges that were denied to student assistants as a de facto policy. He fixed her with a flat look that reminded her disconcertingly of a leopard defending its kill.

"What — " it took her a moment to find her voice " — Gavin? What are you doing?" Her words were more reflex than anything else. There was no misinterpreting the situation. The poor girl had been trying to scream this whole time, and he was denying her even that small dignity. Anger began to curl through Ms. Wilcox's shock, bright red seeping through the gray fog of her mind with striking clarity. Her own younger sister had been assaulted, when they were both teens, by a man old enough to know better. He, too, had been callous in the execution of his selfish desires. In a steel-girded tone Val had never heard her teacher use before, even in class, Ms. Wilcox said, "Get off her, you son of a bitch. Right now."

Slowly, Val felt him release her wrists. Pain arced through them as blood began to circulate with excruciating slowness through her veins. But his legs, still on either side of her hips, tensed as if he were readying himself to spring.

"You're making a terrible mistake."

"Get — away — from *Val*."

She saw his eyes flick towards the drawer where the carving supplies were kept for woodwork. *He wouldn't —*

He was.

Fearscape by Nenia Campbell

Val screamed a wordless protest, grabbing him by the ankle with both arms and pulling hard. His eyes widened almost comically as the ground slid out from under him. All the air in his lungs exploded out of him in a painful-sounding wheeze as he slammed against the floor. Val was on him in an instant, punching, kicking, and clawing, not giving him time to recover.

Which he did. He was quite a bit stronger than she thought. He tried to push her off, but she was clinging to his shirt with her nails, pinching flesh as well as fabric. He made a noise that sounded like a cross between a growl, a gasp, and a laugh.

Val went for his eyes and he turned his head, so her blow caught him beneath the jaw. Raw stripes appeared in the wake of her fingers, already welling up with blood. "I suggest you stop now," he said, catching her hand as she cocked her arm back for another strike. "Before you regret this."

"Don't touch me."

Val gouged at his hand, yanking at the same time. She heard him hiss. Then his fingers closed around her wrist and he gave a vicious tug of his own — she felt the pain ricochet up her arm, spurring the neural equivalent of an echo chamber in her shoulder socket — as he brought her arm behind her back.

Ms. Wilcox had managed to get to the phone, which Gavin evidently hadn't had the foresight to tamper with. She was calling the police. They would be here in three minutes. That might not be soon enough. Val snapped her head back, hitting him in the forehead and eliciting a growl. Behind her back, the pressure on her wrist tightened to where she feared the bones might snap.

He didn't speak right away, though she felt his rapid breathing stir her sweat-soaked hair. "I am trying to make this as civil as possible, but you are forcing my hand, Val."

He paused.

"Unless this is what you want, of course. But somehow I do not think this is the case, anymore than a fox, half-mad with fear, gnaws at its own limbs by preference when caught in a steel trap." She shuddered at the terrible appropriateness of that analogy.

"Come with me," he said, "and I will teach you things the likes of which all men dream but none dare. You're as bestial as I, my dear, in your own artless way — but you need a hunter just as I need my quarry. Freedom quickly grows stale on the tongue without the added spice of imprisonment, and you'll never want for anything, as long as you submit to me in all ways."

Words tumbled from her lips like blocks of ice. "You're insane."

"Is that a no?"

"It's a go to hell!"

"Then what if instead of going after you I went after someone you hold dear? Would you resist me then? Or would you play my way in exchange for their well-being?"

Val stiffened.

"You would. You would, wouldn't you? Interesting. I'll be sure to keep that in mind."

She jerked as if his words had been a physical blow. "Don't you dare! Leave them alone you — you — you *bastard*. Leave them alone or — or I'll *make* you leave them alone."

"So fierce," he said approvingly, "And so protective. Yes, I think I like this side to you."

"I mean it!" Desperation rendered her voice shrill. "This

isn't a game. You can't do this to people. You can't play with them like they're pawns."

"That's where you're wrong," he said calmly. "I can."

And he pulled her back by her chin and kissed her on the mouth, which was still open with shock. Once she had sufficiently recovered her senses she bit him. He bit back harder, and she felt his tongue sweep the inside of her mouth to lap at their commingling blood. Val gagged and tried to pull away, only to gasp as pain flared down her shoulders at the renewed pressure on her arms.

"You can't win against me — and you're only going to hurt yourself, doing that."

She could see Ms. Wilcox approaching. "He's crazy," Val choked out to her, "he thinks he's an animal — he drinks people's *blood*. Please, you have to tell someone — he's sick."

And Val saw a strange expression flicker over her teacher's face; she was in no state to put words to it, but it frightened her. Gavin's grip tightened on her wrists, making her gasp, but he didn't speak.

"Tell her, you bastard," she sobbed, "tell her about the *savanna*, and the killings. Tell her everything."

"I have no idea what you're talking about," he said softly. "Poor Val."

"What does that mean? What are you doing?"

Before he could answer, he was yanked off her by a member of the Derringer Police Department — a tall, robust black man who made no effort to be gentle. And then Val felt Ms. Wilcox's hands on her shoulders, her voice in her ear asking her if she was all right. But all she could taste was the blood, and all she could see were those eyes.

And then everything went black.

Fearscape by Nenia Campbell

Epilogue

The entire situation created quite the scandal for both the school and Val's family. Gavin's trial was the biggest thing to happen to the small town in years, and highly publicized. There was no escape. Val spent the entire summer in her room.

Right before the trial began, the Kimbles received a check in the mail for an extravagant sum of money. Though signed, it was clearly from a sock puppet bank account, as was the return address of the nameless card tied to the red roses which accompanied them. There was no question in anyone's mind who they were from — or why.

Val's mother pleaded with Val once more. She begged her daughter to take the witness stand and testify against the man who had betrayed her. But the thought of standing in a big room crammed with people telling them what he'd done while he *looked* at her the entire time, secretly reveling in her misery — well, that was too horrible to even contemplate.

Her mother cried, and threw a plate against the wall. She then set fire to the roses, snapping the stems and singing the card, and then sent the mess back to the return address.

Val's refusal to testify came as a huge blow for the

prosecution. So much of the evidence was based on her word alone that there was hardly enough to build a case without her testimony. She knew this because she had happened across the trial while channel-surfing, and sat, frozen, when the camera panned to the object of her many nightmares.

He was wearing a three-piece suit and sporting a bit of designer stubble, and looked so handsome it hurt. Val stared, stunned and heartbroken, as he sat there, with a studied attempt at solemnity, while his lawyer brought up his academic scholarship, his acclaim among the chess community, and his living alone, on his own, paying his own bills in age when most teenagers still couldn't calculate a tip.

By contrast, the lawyer portrayed her as a raving lunatic. He claimed that Val had built a delusional adolescent fantasy around his client, and then gotten violently angry when he couldn't live up to her expectations. The fact that she hadn't appeared in court to make her case, he argued, seemed very suspicious, especially when paired with her family's silence.

Ms. Wilcox had agreed to testify, as had Beatrice Cooper, but neither of them had helped much. Ms. Cooper hadn't seen Gavin chasing Val, she only knew that Val had been deathly frightened — traumatized, was the word she used — to the point where she had practically been rendered mute. Could it have been possible that Val had been running from an imaginary terror? Ms. Cooper conceded that yes, she supposed this was possible, albeit unlikely.

Ms. Wilcox's testimony was even worse. She claimed that the situation in the art room had just "seemed" wrong, which the defense pounced on, ultimately boxing her into a corner where she was forced to admit that Gavin hadn't actually hurt her, and that Val's behavior had been rather erratic and odd. She recalled an incident a few weeks before when Gavin had, concernedly, told Val she was acting "strange."

(I can make you feel whatever I want)

That was the final blow.

He planned it, she thought. *He planned it all.*

Gavin ended up winning the criminal case. The charges were dropped, the lawyers paid. A couple weeks later, a "for sale" sign appeared in his yard. Other scandals received their fifteen minutes of spotlight and infamy, and the incident between Val and Gavin was gradually forgotten.

That is, forgotten by everyone except Val.

Fearscape by Nenia Campbell

Val grew from a wiry, bright-eyed fourteen-year-old to a slender, solemn seventeen-year-old, Her hair darkened from orange to brown, and her once-prominent freckles began to fade. People who never noticed her before suddenly began to take notice, to take a second look — and she withered a little under each double-take.

Because every time someone got close to her, she felt his warm breath on her face, his hands on her skin, his voice in her ear — like slow-acting poison he remained latent in her blood, killing her slowly from within. When he had left town, it seemed he'd taken a piece of her with him.

(Can you feel the ties that bind us? Can you feel them tightening? Because I can, and they're so tight that I can scarcely breathe.)

She would never be the same.

For nearly three years, she remained isolate. Eventually, during the summer before her senior year, she agreed to go out with James — and this quiescence was due more to weariness than any real affection. He had asked her out for the first time just a few months after the incident. Repeat requests were made, periodically, every few months or so. Each time, it was harder to say "no." She was so torn up inside that such devotion, even if it was misplaced, made her feel obligated.

So one day, she said "yes."

James might have been disconcerted to know how often Gavin occupied his girlfriend's thoughts (because the answer was far more often than James himself did). Sometimes, thinking about the dark-haired man with the eyes of ice made her cry. Sometimes she would lie still and stare wide-eyed at the ceiling. Other times, though — well, she didn't quite know what she felt, only that the sheer, cutting intensity of it was like a silver dagger in her breast.

Because in spite of what her parents, the therapists, the school, and the policemen, and all her friends said, she was still very much afraid. Because they had not had him speaking into their ears with that deep, gravelly voice that seemed to transcend all reason. They had not felt the determination in those hands. They had not seen the cruelty in those eyes.

If they had, they would know as well as she did that he would come back for her one day.

And, as she had with James, Val lived in constant terror of

the fact that this time she might not be strong enough to say "no."

■□■□■□■

I buy a red rose every morning, and every night I consign it to the fire.

One rose, for every day they keep us apart, ever rising anew from the smoldering ashes like a vengeful phoenix that has just tasted blood.

One rose, to symbolize the fluid shift from beauty to detritus, from love to hatred.

One rose, as fresh as blood spilled on snow — but still nowhere near as lovely as you.

Someday you will blossom, and when that day comes I will find you. And then, my wayward beauty, we will play a different kind of chess. A variant with people, instead of pawns. A variant of love and war, of life and death. Because I know what makes you burn now — what makes you fight. I know you aren't quite as good at resisting me as you would like to believe.

You can choose to see me as your prison or your pasture. Either way, you will wear my bridle. But I warn you now — my expectations are higher; I hope, for your sake, that you can say the same. Because I've decided that if I can't have you, nobody else shall, either.

I'm waiting for you.

Fearscape by Nenia Campbell

Acknowledgments

There are so many people I'd like to thank that I'd probably run out of paper if I tried, so I'll do my best.

McQuinn: For plying me with facts about legal proceedings and criminal trials. You have the right to remain awesome!

Louisa: For making a cover that displays as much beauty and talent as she, herself, possesses.

Kendal: For ~~beating me over the head about~~ enlightening me on the difference between "nauseous" and "nauseated," and other niggling little errors~~, such as why using ellipses warrants years of painful suffering in grammar hell~~.

Printed in Germany
by Amazon Distribution
GmbH, Leipzig